BONUS TIME

by James F. La Marca

RoseDog🐾Books

PITTSBURGH, PENNSYLVANIA 15222

RoseDog Books
701 Smithfield Street
Pittsburgh, PA 15222
Visit our website at www.rosedogbookstore.com

ISBN: 978-1-4349-8812-6
eISBN: 978-1-4349-7807-3

Now that the project has come to fruition, I must thank my wonderful support system-my family. My daughter Joanne never tired of my asking for guidance, at least she didn't admit to it ! My talented daughter Sharon, lent her skills and her time as the illustrator of the cover of this book.My son in law Sam who is going to make this book available on his web site. My grand-children Scott and Ashley who assisted me when i needed them. Every house needs teenagers ! My son in law Tyler repeatedly read page after page to help me edit this book soon to be a film. I applaud his patience and concentration and envy it as well and to my wife Lynn who had to listen to me for 18 months while watching rewrite after rewrite pile up on the dining room table and of course I want to thank my good friends without their stories I would not have had mine.

This book is dedicated to my life long friend Domenick Bove who motivated me from the beginning here on earth and later from a much higher place. Dom this ones for you !

Introduction

Is time running out? It's almost the ninth inning.
For some old guys, maybe! But for these guys, it's the beginning.
You live your life, the kids are grown,
And now the kids have kids of their own.
The sight grows dim, the step becomes slow,
But you are still here with maybe a couple of years to go.
Sometimes life, it stops on a dime!
Not for this crew, they're on bonus time.
They will use these last few years
to remove an evil man who has caused many fears
Let's do it, they said, or go out trying.
We are on <u>Bonus Time</u>. Who cares about dying?

1. ANOTHER PLEASANT BUT BORING SATURDAY

Jim sat in his usual Saturday morning seat in the rear of the diner. He was always the first one to arrive for the weekly Saturday morning breakfast with, as he referred to them, the guys. They had been together for more than thirty years, through marriages, divorces, and lately even their children's divorces. They'd seen sicknesses together, family tragedies and plenty of celebrations too. Now it seemed that mostly what they shared, besides these Saturday conclaves, was an endless array of prescription drugs to treat all the usual afflictions of men their ages – from high blood pressure to low urine flow and everything in between. Jim gulped down his Atenol and Fosparil and waited for the guys to arrive.

Dom was the second to arrive. He was still a formidable presence at 6 feet, 230 pounds. Even at the age of 72 and slowed down by an assortment of pills from Losortan for high blood pressure to Terrazosin for blood flow and the many more meds too numerous to mention. Even with all of his ailments he still didn't take anyone's bullshit. Bad enough he had to listen to his wife Marie! Anyone else who opened a mouth to him, he would verbally tear apart. Dom, a Korean War vet, has five children, ten grandchildren, many of them named Domenick or Dominique. Dom was a survivor of no fewer than six operations, the most major being quadruple bypass to the most recent knee replacement. He was retired 10 years from the largest tobacco company in America.

The third to arrive was Tommy, 5 feet 9 inches, 188 pounds, an ex-Marine, 70 years old, married father of three, no grandchildren. Tom was a real bulldog and Dom's favorite verbal sparring partner. No matter what the topic, whether it was the proper way to pour a beer to the way the President was handling social security, the were diametricly opposed. Tom had a fierce temper, proved by the loss of one of his eyes more than

50 years ago after a fight with a sailor. He was retired 10 years from the Faberge Cosmetics Company.

The fourth to arrive was Phil, 68 years old, 6 feet one inch, 240 pounds. A veteran of heart bypass and prostate cancer, he was being treated with an assortment of pills from Capacartia to Lorenzipan. Phil strove for peace and tranquility and rarely got either one. He was a divorced father of two, grandfather of three, and still worked n his son David's electrical contracting business.

The fifth arrival was Billy, perhaps the most gentle of the guys. Bill is 68 years old, 5 feet 11 inches, 200 pounds. He's a married father of three, grandfather of five and the former owner of the diner that the guys now call their "office." Bill spoke four languages fluently—English, Spanish, Italian and Greek. He very rarely got angry and was basically the peacemaker of the group. Bill was being treated with Diaval, Crestor and Mobic.

The sixth to arrive was Steve, 74 years old, 5 feet 9 inches, 188 pounds. His medical resume included six stents and a new hip, which he received two years ago. He is the father of two and the grandfather of two, recently widowed and on Plavix, Rampail, Coregser and Simvastation. As close as the guys were, Steve in many ways was a mystery to all of them. As long as the guy had known him, it was never clear to them how Steve made his living. For as long as they knew Steve, he insisted he was retired, but no one ever knew from what and none of them wanted to ask. Steve was the guy you didn't want to cross. Jim remembered a time twenty years ago when he put his nose into a problem of a friend that coincidently involved friends of Steve. Steve came to Jim's house, looked him in the eye and said, "Jim, I love you like a brother. In fact, I love you more than my brother. But if I had to kill you, I would."

Jim was always the first to arrive. He was the glue that held these guys together for over thirty years! Of course, there were ten of them then. Petey, Pat, Henry and Mickey had passed. Jim is 6 feet, 1 inch, 236 pounds and, as he loved to say, of rompin', stompin', death and destruction. He is 68 years old, perhaps the most vocal of a very vocal group, married with 2 children and 4 grandchildren. He liked to sing, tell jokes and write. Billy loved to steal his routines and in jest present them as his own. This would amuse Jim to no end. Jim's strongest point seemed to be his ability to talk the guys into doing some pretty crazy things like taking the upstairs room at Viola's Restaurant and turning it into a poker palace where the guys cut every pot. Jim five years before had colon cancer, but so far, he was a survivor.

You have now met the senior six, an unlikely group of aging guys that are about to set the world on its ear and the only thing that could possibly stop them is their medication!

2. THE MEETING

As the guys were making themselves comfortable sitting at the round table in the rear of the diner, Dom said, "Guys, I have some good news for you. My daughter is going to have a baby," to which Billy replied, "Let me guess. If it's a boy, they will name it Domenick, and if it's a girl, Dominique. That will make it unanimous. All of your five children will have a child named Domenick or Dominique."

Dom looked at Billy and said, "Bill, it is all about respect." And Dom was right. He and his wife Marie managed to keep the family tight, just as it was in the 50's when they grew up. It wasn't long before the subject returned to the usual descriptions of medicine and pills and who was taking what. Jim thought this was boring and depressing and changed the subject with a series of what ifs. What if someone offered you a million dollars, but you couldn't watch television for two years? What if a beautiful young thing walked up to you and offered super sex? Bill immediately yelled he'd take the soup. The table erupted into a long, roaring laugh and all eyes in the diner focused on them. A guy in the corner wanted to know if they had ordered the happy meal. Phil then stopped the laughter quickly with his hypothetical, "What if you knew you were dying, what would you do?"

Everyone again turned solemn. Leave it to Phil to bring everyone down to earth or, maybe, just down. It was an interesting question, though, and somehow it led the guys back to some very familiar conversational territory. You see, these guys were "old school." While they disagreed about a lot of things, the one unfailing consensus among them was that the America they lived in today did not resemble the America they grew up in and loved in the 1940S AND 50S. Caught in a time warp. That was it. That was what they all were. Stuck: guys in their 60S and 70S trapped in the 1950S. High tech stuff? Apart from their 50 inch high def flat screens, they mostly hated it. Cell phones? Oh, maybe two of them carried them. Texting? Twittering? Forget it. In fact, Jim had a rule at his house: when the grandkids came over, they had to check their phones at the door.

Of all of them, Dom perhaps took the time warp stuff closest to heart. He used to wonder out loud if all those guys WHO fought and died in World War II somehow were watching from above, from heaven or hell or wherever they were. And what if they were watching? What did they see in the America they left behind, the America they died to defend? More to the point, what did they think of what they saw? How did today's America make them feel? Hell! Even English was becoming a second language and the country that they fought and died for was being trampled on. How would they feel? Billy would always remark, "When are we going to show the world that we're just not going to take it anymore!"

Steve had the perfect solution, at least he thought so! "Let us single out one of these countries that are always denouncing us as the Great Satan and bomb the shit out of them. This will serve notice to the rest of the world."

Phil thought the only answer was isolation. "Let's take care of our own," he would say. "Let the rest of the world fend for themselves."

Tom blurted out, "You guys are all full of shit. All you do is talk. There hasn't been a fresh idea that has come out of these meetings in thirty years. In fact, our rhetoric is as old as our bodies and just as stale."

Jim thought to himself that Tom was right. All the guys did was talk! First about their medicines, and then about how abused America was. Another thing that was consistent was that although they represented many nationalities in their heritages, they were all fiercely patriotic and proud to be an American.

Phil then again said, "I didn't hear an answer to my question."

Jim then said, "Nobody's dying here, at least right now."

Then Steve chimed in with, "Did you guys ever watch the Classic Move Channel and see the great movies made in the 1940's and 1950's and realize that all these people are now dead! They were handsome, the women were beautiful, all were full of vitality and now they are dead!"

3. THE BUS DRIVERS AND THEIR BORING LIVES

Tommy looks at Steve and says, "What is your point?"

Steve answered, "My point is obvious. We all have to die! The rich, the poor, the beautiful, the ugly, the good and bad of us. We all have to go."

Jim thought for a moment and then added his two cents. "It's inevitable," he said. "Death is a destiny we all have in common. We know that somewhere lurking out there is a disease with our name on it, or perhaps a condition we already have. Something has got to get us sooner or later. Let's just hope it's later. The great, most optimistic thing as I see it is how we go out! Preferably on our terms."

"That's a beautiful thought," Dom said, "but very few people go out on their own terms."

Billy announced, "Breakfast is over. I promised my wife Joyce I'd pick up the grandchildren and bring them home."

Dom said, "I know the feeling. Sometimes I think I should paint my SUV yellow and write 'school bus' on the side."

Phil remarked, "Look what we've been reduced to—a bunch of boring, old men whose highlight of their day is probably picking up their grandchildren."

The guys break up with a series of, "I'll call you during the week," remarks, and then Jim saying, "Same place. Same time. Next week."

The following Saturday came around very quickly. Jim had a Chinese friend who always said, "When you're twenty years old, your life goes at twenty miles an hour. When you're forty years old, at forty miles an hour. And when you're sixty years old, at sixty miles an hour." The minutes, the weeks, were just flying right by him. In the past fleeting week, he'd had an idea and wondered about the reaction of the guys when he sprung it on them. They would probably think he was crazy, but that was nothing new. They always greeted his ideas that way and then somehow, someway, he was almost always able to convince them. As all the guys filed in, they sat at a round table and ordered their coffee—four decaf, two regular and an assortment of egg dishes. After a little light conversation, everyone finished their breakfast and Jim wondered who was going to be the first to mention a doctor or medication or trouble pissing or some other health related subject, and then probably Dom would comment on some political headline, followed by Tommy's rebuttal of any point Dom was trying to make. Sure enough, Phil started with the amount of times he had to get up last night to pee and he thought a lot of it was caused by his blood pressure medicine. To which Dom said, "If it wasn't for you getting up to pee every half-hour, you would never get any exercise."

All the guys laugh, but in reality, they all got up during the night to pee, but just not quite as frequently as Phil. Dom changed gears and started talking politics, the Mideast and the Tea Party rally that he had been attending.

"Yeah," Tom said. "A bunch of old men getting their rocks off and telling each other old war stories."

Jim thought, "We're off to the races. They're at it again."

Billy, forever the peacemaker, said, "Why don't you guys knock it off? Can't we all ever agree on something?"

Steve said, "Yeah! We all think you're funny looking."

Jim decided to try to move the conversation in another direction. He reminded the guys of the conversation they had last Saturday about how disgusted they were waiting for America to assert itself and how boring THE GUYS HAD BECOME: ALL TALK AND NO ACTION.

Phil piped in with, "Last week, as usual, we discussed many topics from America, to dying, to how boring we have all become."

Jim said, "Just a thought. You know all of us in the last five years have had some sort of major surgery. We are all on medication, but otherwise somewhat healthy. The way I look at it, we are on 'bonus time'."

Billy says, "So what is your point?"

"I'll tell you my point," Jim replies. Collectively, the guys sigh and in unison cry, "Here it comes."

4. LET'S FISH,
"I'VE GOT THE HOOK"

The guys were used to Jim's setups. Tom looked at Jim and said, "You got the hook in us! Now are you going to reel us in, like the time twenty years ago you almost convinced us that we could make a porno movie, have fun and even make a few dollars. Remember that!"

Dom said, "Remember it, my wife still won't let me forget it!"

"Okay, here's my point," Jim said. "Remember Phil brought up how if we were dying, how would we like to go out?"

Phil interrupted. "That's not exactly what I said, but go on."

"Okay!" Jim began to explain. "I've been thinking about all these what ifs that we always seem to get around to, but what if all of us could dictate the terms we go out on?"

Steve looks at Jim and says, "You mean, we pick the way we die?"

Jim replies, "Something like that."

"Well, don't leave us hanging!" Phil stated. "What diabolical scheme are you planning now?"

"Phil, my friend, for thirty years," Jim said, "what if all of us had an opportunity to do something very special? The downside is you would probably die doing it. But then the upside is you would die a hero doing something very special for your country, which until this very moment, no one has been able to do."

"What's that?" Dom said. "Reducing unemployment."

"Very funny!" Jim said, and all the guys laughed.

Tom said, "Are you going to share with us? What's this great, patriotic thing that we can possibly do?"

Jim said, "Let us leave this for next week. Right now, let us all enjoy our breakfast."

"Oh!" said Steve. "You are going to keep us in suspense."

Jim replied, "I do not think I am ready to tell you q-tips yet. I have to give it more thought."

The guys finish their breakfast, exchange pleasantries and, as always, depart to the usual chorus of "same time, next week." Meanwhile, Jim's mind is spinning: how will I tell them what I want to do without them thinking here's another fine mess our buddy is getting us into.

5. YESTERDAY

Jim was reflecting on his youth and thinking of how similar he and his friends had been in their upbringing. Tom was born in Brooklyn. He was the first child of Mike and Eleanor Kellerher, an Irish father and an Italian mother who were to eventually have two more children and, as was the custom in those days, later move to Queens, their own home and a better life for the children. Tom and Jim had been friends the longest, actually going back to their preteens. Tom had a fierce temper and would fight at the drop of a hat. The kids would refer to him (though of course not to his face) as "a walking time bomb." Tom was very industrious as a child, holding as many as three jobs at a time. There wasn't a guy on the baseball team that Jim and Tom played on that didn't think eventually Tom would join the Marines—and he did. When he left the Marines in the mid 1960s, Jim introduced him to his wife, Myrtle, with whom he had three children.

Jim and Dom had worked together at the same tobacco company, and in 1967, Jim and Dom arranged an interview with a mutual friend who worked at the Faberge Cosmetics Company. Tom got the job and despite his volatility, he became Regional Sales Manager, where he held the job until he retired.

Dom Faella's parents were born in Italy, but were determined to have their children born in America. Dom was raised in Queens, had two brothers and two sisters, worked very hard as a kid, first in construction, then at his father's beer and soda distributorship. Dom was the youngest in the family and he followed both his brothers into the Unites States Army where all three boys fought during the Korean Conflict. Upon leaving the service, Dom met his wife Marie, married and had five children of his own.

Billy Pappas escaped Greece with his sister when the Germans invaded. Bill got to America at the tender young age of eight. His older sister, who was in her mid-teens, married very young and she and her husband settled in Astoria Queens, where they helped to raise Bill. In his late teens in Astoria at a Greek church event, he met Joyce, whose father owned the diner the guys now met in. When Joyce's parents passed, Billy took over the diner. Billy was the father of two boys and a girl. In 2002, Bill sold the diner and retired. The year before, he had lost his son-in-law in a tragic car accident.

Phil Stein was born in Brooklyn as one of three brothers. His father was an electrician, so he followed into the electrician's union, met his wife Gail, married and had two children. Phil's parents were Jewish, so as he said, "I guess that makes me Jewish." Phil never really practiced his faith although he made sure his son David celebrated his Bar Mitzvah. Phil left the electrician's union to start a contracting business with his brother, Max. Now divorced, he helps his son David in David's electrical contracting business.

Steve Busso was born in Brooklyn in 1935 to Italian parents who'd arrived just six months earlier. There, growing up with his two brothers in the Italian conclave of Bensonhurst, Steve spent most of his teenage years hustling on the streets of Brooklyn. He first met his wife, Sabina, when the two of them were 12. They married 10 years later and had two kids, a boy and a girl. Almost from the beginning of his marriage, Steve was a bit of a wild man, staying out late, coming home when he pleased and hanging out with the city's most notorious wiseguys. Steve, now a widower, has calmed down a lot in his old age and from time to time can be seen at St. Joseph's Church attending mass.

Jim thought one thing was clear—not one of the guys was born with a silver spoon in HIS mouth. Jim was born in East New York, Brooklyn, the only child of Mr. and Mrs. Joseph Canova. His teenage years were mainly spent playing ball. He

met his wife Lynn at 18. They were married and at 21 had started a family. At 23, they had two children. Jim worked at the
same tobacco company Dom did, but at the age of 38, left to
open his own tobacco distributorship business, which had a
very short life span. He later worked in the advertising business, selling and creating ads, which he retired from at the age
of 67.

Now all their lives came together. They even socialized frequently with their wives, but Jim thought that they all to a man
had become stagnant, bitter, and perhaps just tired of living.
This is the ingredients that had spurred his latest fantasy. The
question was, will the guys buy it?

6. ARE THE FISH BITING?

Saturday again was here and the guys were at their same table. The breakfast order was given and the usual kibitzing with the waitress was over.

"Now!" Billy said. "Jim, are you ready to give us the answer to last week's riddle?"

"Let's see!" Dom said. "One of the clues was 'do something for your country'!"

"Yeah," Phil said. "Another clue was, 'you might die doing it'!"

Tom said, "Let's not forget it's something no one has been able to do!"

Steve remembered another clue was, "You might die a hero!"

Finally Dom said, "Okay, no one has gotten it! You want to share the answer with us?"

Jim said, "Are you ready for this?"

He paused, not so much for dramatic effect but because he almost couldn't believe what he was about to propose, what he was about to ask his best friends in the world to do. It was crazy, no doubt about that. But no crazier than some of the stuff they'd done 50 years ago. His heart started to race. He could feel it in his chest. He took a deep breath. And then the words spilled out.

"Guys," he said, "We are going to get Bin Laden!"

Dead silence around the table, then uncontrolled laughter. Phil laughed so hard he fell out of his seat and wet his pants. Then the laughter subsided and they looked at each other. They realized that one of them was not laughing. It was Jim. Could it be he was serious? No, not even he could think that six guys in the twilight of their lives, all on some type of daily medication, could even entertain the thought of attacking the Amish, let alone Usama Bin Laden, the world's most famous fugitive terrorist.

Jim said, "Okay, guys, laugh! When you finish laughing, get up, get in your cars, pick up your grandchildren, go home, take your medicine, listen to your wife tell you about all the things you should be doing around the house, or dare to be great! I leave that to you. Chew on it, digest it, and I'll see you next week, same time."

With that, he stood up and quietly walked out.

The guys looked at each other in stunned silence. Jim walked to his car thinking the guys were probably talking about him and having a good laugh. At least, he now let them know what he had in mind. He didn't have to divulge the actual plan that he was still formulating. When the time is right he would tell them the strange string of events that led him to believe he just might know where Bin Laden is. The guys didn't know that Jim had started researching this project months ago after an extremely curious conversation Jim had with a Pakistani acquaintance who calls himself Stoney.

Jim had already researched how this plan he was formulating could be carried out. He even knew what the consequences could be. But he was getting ahead of himself. His basic first step and probably the hardest was to convince the guys. Meanwhile, as Jim predicted, once he left the diner, the guys discussed the zaniness of Jim's new fantasy. That day they left the diner thinking they were being set up for another one of Jim's practical jokes. Jim's plan so far would at least get them to the target area. He also researched how once there, they would carry out America's revenge. The guys had no idea how extensive Jim's plans were. In the short term Jim's job would be to wear down and persuade his friends the job could be done, but perhaps not without a price. Jim had solid information provided by Stoney, whose brother was the head of the ISI in Pakistan. He had substantiated through countless hours of research at the library that what he had been told by Stoney had at least a 95% chance of being true and that Bin Laden was being kept alive and guarded by the Pakistani army at a military base on the Pakistan/Western Afghanistan border.

7. THE SKEPTICISM

Here it was, Saturday already. Boy! The Chinese were right—the older you get, the faster time goes. Jim headed to the diner and when he got there he couldn't believe what he saw. For the first time in years, all the guys were there ahead of him. Jim was sure this was by design. They probably in fact most likely were discussing last week's meeting, trying to determine whether their friend Jim had finally gone completely crazy.

"Good morning!" Jim bellowed out to all the guys. "Did you notice last week we didn't even discuss medication or current events? You know why? Because I gave us something to think about and instead of bellyaching, a reason for living."

To which Dom immediately replied, "Are you taking Viagra, because I think it went in the wrong direction. You sound like you have a stiff brain."

"Dom!" Jim said. "You are a funny man!"

"Funny, how?" Dom said. "I'm here to amuse you."

"Don't start that shit," Jim said. "Leave that to Joe Pesci."

Phil jumped in and said, "The last time I even had a fight, I was sixteen years old."

Tom said, "Look, I've fought. I even lost an eye in a fight. But that was fifty years ago."

"Look!" Dom said. "In a toe to toe fight at this point in my life, Marie could take me."

Steve's take on the situation was, "Is there a contract on this guy? I only work with a contract."

Bill said, "I got an idea. Let's take him some takeout food

from here! That will kill him."

Jim began to get irritated. He chastised the guys, telling them, "Go ahead and laugh if you want. Grow old and become a burden to your wife and kids and get caught by some disease that's probably shadowing you right now as we speak, or try to achieve the unachievable and at worst, go out like a hero."

"Come on!" Bill said. "This hasn't been accomplished by the most trained people on Earth, and even if you were serious, it's impossible."

"Let's get this clear from the start," Jim barked. "I am serious."

Dom protested, "Who here is in shape to even attack Barney Frank, let alone Bin Laden?"

Steve continued to protest that he "doesn't do anything without a contract."

Tom had his say. "This is a great fantasy, but could you imagine us being trained and armed? And how would we even get to Afghanistan or Pakistan or wherever they hell they say he's hiding?"

Phil said, "You know, if this was possible, I'd be in, only because I'm sick and tired of being sick and tired! I've been depressed and I know you guys are aware of it. So if you really thought this could be done, count me in. If I go out, it will be on a high note, not as a beaten man."

Jim said, "I have some great information as to the whereabouts of this monster."

Tom almost jumps out of his chair. "You have information? Give me a break."

"Tom, I have good information that I'll share with all of you later. And that's if you take this seriously!" Jim said. "And furthermore, why should we leave this problem to our grandchildren? At least we are all on bonus time."

Phil muttered, "Talk about time. It's time to piss again. Do they have bathrooms in that part of the world?"

"Phil, even if they don't have bathrooms, they have a lot of big rocks you can go behind!" Jim assured.

Billy finally spoke. "How would we get there?"

Jim tried to answer. "They must have tours. Maybe not

Perillo, but someone does offer a tour and I'm almost positive there is a tour company in Afghanistan that offers tours. In fact, I remember reading they had a website: www.afghanlogistics.com."

Dom said, "I have a question. How may I ask are we going to get in even reasonable shape?"

"That is easy," Jim quipped. "Remember the gym I belonged to, run by my friend Nelson? He just stared new classes for seniors. It's called Nelson's Senior Boot Camp. I'm sure if I asked him, he would agree to train us in private, after hours."

"How about the arms, genius?" Billy asked. "How are you going to arrange that?"

"Billy, my boy, to tell you the truth, I'm still working on that, but remember," Jim said, "David slew the giant with a slingshot. And correct me if I'm wrong, but it was in that part of the world. Listen, guys. Eat your breakfast and I make one request of all OF you—this conversation STAYS right here."

"I have one more thing to say," said Dom. "I can't believe you are fucking serious and we are even considering this. I think we are all a few cards short of a full deck."

The seniors walked out of the diner a little dumbfounded, but at least their creative friend had given them something else to think about instead of thinking of medication and growing old. They could at least become Walter Mitty for awhile and dream of being a hero.

8. THE DECISION

The following Saturday as everyone is filing into the diner, Jim is thinking they will probably tell him to go fuck himself. He is sure they probably discussed this amongst themselves and Dom, the loudest, would have convinced them that this was the craziest of all the crazy ideas he has ever heard of. Then Jim thought, if Dom felt that way, wouldn't Tommy take the exact opposite view? So maybe he had a fifty-fifty chance.

The guys approach Jim at the table and Tom cracks, "Hey! John Wayne is here first as usual."

Jim, a little agitated, looks at Tom and the guys and says, "Is that the best you could come up with?"

"How about this?" Bill says. "In Pakistan or Afghanistan or wherever the hell you want to take us, do they have Preparation H? Maybe I can finally get rid of you hemorrhoids!"

Jim, again showing his agitation, says, "You guys can have breakfast by yourselves."

He gets up to leave and Dom yells, "Where the hell are you going? To invade Cuba?"

Everyone laughs and Jim sits back down with the guys. As he sits, he decides to get right down to business and asks, "Have you guys thought about our project?"

Dom immediately bellows, "How does *your* fucking project always become *our* fucking project?"

Jim immediately feels like Dom's reply was not a good omen and braced himself to be let down.

"Listen," Tom said. "You certainly gave us a lot to think

about, and if you can get us some convincing evidence that this is not just another one of your fantasies, you might be pleasantly surprised."

Jim responded quickly, "I have plenty of evidence, but first, if you are in—and I mean definitely in—place your hand on the table, palm down."

Dom looked at Jim and, to Jim's astonishment, placed his hand on the table palm down. He had a grin from ear to ear and chirped, "You didn't expect that, did you?"

Phil needed no prodding. His hand found the back of Dom's, followed by Billy's, than a slight hesitation and Tommy's hand found Billy's. That left Steve. Jim figured from the beginning that if there was a weak link, it was Steve because no one could ever really figure Steve.

Steve protested, "This is against everything I believe in—working without a contract."

But a minor miracle, Steve's hand landed on top of Tommy's. That left Jim. The thought occurred briefly to the guys, was this all an elaborate setup for one of Jim's jokes? Then Jim's hand landed on the back of Steve's as he yelled, "Bonus time!"

9. YES AND NO AND THAT'S A DEFINITE MAYBE

Later that night, the thought occurred to Jim that maybe the guys were just giving him lip service. Maybe they thought this was a thousand to one shot, this idea would ever get off the ground and just maybe they were going along with him just to shut him up! But now, at least he had a kind of buy-in from them. They'd said yes. All of them. And more than that, they'd laid their hands down on that Formica table, a gesture that told Jim they were willing to lay down their lives – for him, and for the America they loved. Now it was up to him. Sure, he'd thought about the outlines of the plan. But now he really had to come through for his guys, just as his guys – against the odds – had come through for him. He had to start some serious planning. If he didn't blow away his buddies the next Saturday at the diner with details of the plan, they might bag it. The next week, if anything, was more important than any of the preceding ones. He had to get working. Fast.

10. THAT'S PAR FOR THE COURSE

The two middle-aged librarians behind the information counter at the Oceanside Library were enjoying their morning coffee and engaging in some idle chit chat when Gladys said to Pat, "Well, we are about to begin another ho-hum day. The same old people will come in, sit behind the computers because they're too cheap to buy them for their own homes. Then in the afternoon when school is over, the kids will stop by to do some research for a school project. Nothing out of the ordinary, nothing exciting."

"Maybe you want Tiger Woods to waltz in here and give you golfing lessons and then take you for a nap at the Holiday Inn!" Pat replied.

Gladys looked at Pat and said, "That's some racy dialogue for a library. And is that what they call it now, a nap?"

Both women giggled, just as they were approached by a tall, dark, hulking figure. Jim was at the counter one minute after the library opened and asked the heavier set of the two ladies where he could find books on Bin Laden, Afghanistan and Pakistan. The heavyset lady stole a quick glance at her coworker Pat, then gave Jim the reference numbers.

As Jim walked away, Gladys said to Pat, "Wow! Did that guy look ominous?"

To which Pat replied, "Gladys, your quest for excitement is overruling your brain and I think you're just hoping that there is something sinister about that man."

"Yeah!" said Gladys. "That guy is at least sixty-five years old. I do not think he needs those books for a term paper."

Jim grabbed four books off the shelves and started to scan the books for information and to get a feel for the land. How these people lived, who actually ran these countries. The answer—if there was one—to all these questions was complex.

Just then, his thoughts strayed to something perhaps equally important to the mission's logisitcs: how could he get himself and the guys in even reasonable shape for the ordeal that lay ahead? Can he talk his friend Nelson into giving them classes after the gym closed? After all, didn't Nelson tell him just last week that he just introduced an exercise class "for seniors only" called Nelson's Boot Camp for Seniors? Jim figured he should go to his buddy's gym and feel him out about training the guys in secret after the gym closed. He also knew he would have to take Nelson into his confidence. Nelson was a former Mr. America. Over 55 years old, that title was won fifteen years ago. Nelse, as Jim called him, was a married father of seventeen. Nelson was a black man of seventy years old, but looked ten years younger. He was 5 feet 10 inches tall, 230 pounds of solid muscle. His physique looked like it was carved out of steel. Jim walked into Nelson's gym and Nelson immediately walked up to him and gave him a ferocious hug. Nelson knew that when Jim belonged to his gym, he liked to kid everyone there and the whole place used to come to life, but that was six years ago. Nelson whispered in Jim's ear that he was about to start one of his Boot Camp for Seniors classes and would appreciate it if Jim would refrain from any comments because the old timers were very sensitive. Nelson remembered! Jim was like a pound of salt looking for an open wound. His past members liked it, even looked forward to it. But these seniors did not know him and Nelson held his breath.

Jim and Nelse had been friends for fifteen years and even though Jim stopped going to the gym after his surgery. Nelse and Jim remained friends and it didn't hurt that Nelse's wife Colleen and Jim's wife Lynn were very close. They even shared the same birthday.

Nelse looked at Jim and said, "What brings you here, brother?"

Jim said, "I can't just stop by and see how my friend is doing?"

"Oh, no!" Nelse said. "I know you. There has got to be a reason."

"All right!" Jim replied. "I was doing some research at the library and now I have to get some information from you!"

"About what?" Nelson asked.

"About something very special," Jim said.

Nelse replied, "I can't wait to hear this, but I will have to. I have a class to conduct. Grab a chair and in about forty-five minutes, we will grab a bottle of green tea and you can tell me all about this very special whatever it is!"

As Nelse walked to the front of his senior class, the words of Yogi Berra came to Jim's mind. "You could see a lot when you observe." Then Jim began to observe the seniors in the class. There were twelve of them, eight women and four men. The men were all George Burns type characters, 5 feet 5 inches, 140 pounds or there about. The women seemed more varied. Some tall and heavy, some actually skinny. The women for some reason looked a lot healthier than the men. Jim always thought as people aged, the women got stronger and the men weaker. Then he thought it wasn't true of his guys. Maybe they lost a half an inch in height to Father Time, but they still looked somewhat rugged and were definitely very feisty. Jim also remembers when he used to pass the old age homes on the boardwalk of Long Beach. Most of the residents were women and the few men that were there were all small and thin. Whatever happened to the football players, the baseball players or basketball players? The sad truth is probably big guys just don't make it. This did not bode well for his crew.

Back to reality, he thought. He was here to watch the class. Nelse had the seniors stretching, running in place and even working out with light weights. Jim felt Nelse would have to turn it up a notch for his guys, especially the cardio. The class ended and Nelse brought Jim back to his office.

Nelse looked at Jim and said, "What are you cooking up now, brother?"

Jim asked, "Nelse, can I trust you to keep a secret? Regardless of how bizarre what I'm going to say might sound."

Nelse said, "I'm hurt that you might even think I couldn't keep a secret."

"All right! Nelse, I need you to run a senior class in secret after hours."

"Why in secret?" Nelse asked.

"I'll tell you why. Because I am one of the six you are going to train because after you put us in reasonable shape, we are going to undertake a plan that some people—and by some people, I mean families, friends—may think is very irrational and then they may try to stop us. And that is why I'm here, my dear friend."

Nelse, grinning broadly, asks, "Are you going to tell me what this master plan is?"

"If I tell you and word gets out, it could ruin our friendship."

"Tell me. C'mon, tell me, brother! Now! I have to know. I'm 70 years old and never betrayed a friend. I'm not going to do it now."

"Yeah!" Jim said. "Like the rest of us, you're on bonus time."

"Bonus time," Nelse thought out loud. "You're right. I'm on bonus time."

Jim then laid it all out to Nelse, every last detail of the plan he's spent the last two months researching and thinking about. Nelse's eyes grew bigger and bigger, his mouth agape. Finally, Nelse broke his silence and said, "You're serious, aren't you?"

"Never more serious in my life," Jim replied.

Nelse said, "I'll train you and your guys on one condition."

"What is that?" Jim asked.

"If you do this thing? If you really think it can be done, I want in. I'd like to go with you, brother."

"Nelson, don't you think you should at least think about it for awhile before you make a commitment?"

Nelson was emphatic. "Count me in."

Jim didn't take long to reply. "You're in," he said. They hugged. "But everything we discussed dies here. Not your wife, your kids—no one is to know!"

11. THE TARGET

A tall, gaunt, forlorn looking man paced back and forth, his eyes deeply sunk into a very thin, narrow face. His body bent, his beard ratty and ragged. He looked far older than his 50 or so years. He was brought to this barren, arid, dusty, unfriendly land by the Pakistani military that convinced him that they were sympathetic to his causes. The Paki generals and Bin Laden knew this refuge was probably the safest place for him. After all, the foolish Americans saw the Pakis as their allies. Years before 9/11, the Pakistanis built a secret military base on the Pakistani border with Afghanistan—a base that was equipped with nuclear weapons that were capable of targeting and hitting their mortal enemy India.

This had become Bin Laden's home for the last seven years. However, the maniacal Bin Laden felt more like a prisoner than a guest. The Paki generals were being paid handsomely by the rich Saudis to keep Bin Laden alive. The C.I.A. and the Pakistani I.S.I knew that this was Bin Laden's refuge. Could it be that the American government was not yet ready to kill Bin Laden? They were afraid of making him a martyr, which might cause a surge of recruits to America's enemies. America knew that the majority of the 9/11 terrorists were Saudis who were trained, no, not in Iran, not in Iraq, but in Pakistan. They also knew that many in the Pakistani military revered him. Bin Laden was aware that this base was the safest place for him. It was safer than some cave or village where eventually someone would talk accidentally or on purpose. Some Afghan woman doing a wash or an Afghan man jealous of the preferential treatment that the Saudi was getting would eventually talk. The frail looking Bin Laden knew he was in failing health and that the Paki doctors were keeping him alive. But for how long, he thought?

12. THE COVER

Jim was transfixed in thought. A lot of bases had to be covered such as, how could they all disappear for a long period of time without arousing some sort of suspicion? Maybe the key to that was in the beginning of the thought! Bases to be covered. It had to be during the summer or maybe the spring. The guys had often discussed renting a tour bus and traveling the country to see a baseball game in every Major League park. The more Jim thought about it, the more he thought this would be the perfect cover. Now his thoughts turned to the three most important challenges: zeroing in on Bin Laden's exact whereabouts; having the firepower to dispense him to the seventy or so virgins his faith promised him for killing innocent men, women and children; and of course, the vehicle or vehicles needed to transport the guys to that Godforsaken area of the world.

The guys would have to start talking it up about the baseball season, the planned trip. Dom would be put in charge of getting the ball rolling, calling all the guys, talking about renting the bus and in general planting the seed. All the wives liked Dom and wouldn't have any reason to doubt that the guys were actually thinking of touring the ballparks. Jim saw just one small problem: Dom's wife Marie was a bigger baseball fan than Dom—and for that matter, she was a bigger fan than all the guys. During the season, come hell or high water (whatever that means), Marie would find a way to watch every New York Yankee ballgame. What if she asked to go on the tour? Nah! Jim thought. Not even Marie would want to be the only woman on a bus with all men.

13. THE NEW RECRUIT

Fred was different from the rest of the guys Jim grew up with. Fred, a confirmed atheist and always a free thinker, went back further with Jim than the senior six. Fred Santos and Jim were kids together. They had seen each other on and off over the last fifty years, but over the last fifteen years, had lost all contact. Then, three years earlier, Jim's wife thought of a great way to surprise Jim for his 65th birthday: find Fred and invite him to the birthday party she was planning. Amazingly Fred was living not far from where he and Jim had grown up in Brooklyn, and yes, Fred and his wife, his fifth wife – would be pleased to be surprise guests at Jim's 65th birthday party. From that day on, the men had stayed close getting together several times a year and talking on the phone at least once a week.

Fred still was an imposing figure at 5 feet 11 inches, 210 pounds. Now a grandfather of two, Fred had survived heart bypass, a valve replacement and prostate cancer, not to mention thousands of insulin shots for diabetes. But in spite of all that, he had a great attitude, never wavered in his beliefs and Jim honestly thought physically and facially, he hadn't changed much. When they were kids, Jim thought that Fred had the best future of all the guys they both grew up with. Fred had graduated Brooklyn Tech High School, went on to Queens College, joined ROTC and eventually became a pilot in the Strategic Air Command. But then something curious happened. Right after the Cuban Missile Crisis, Fred became a peacenik, something the guys that Jim grew up with couldn't understand. Fred marched on Washington, supported many anti-government causes and was very vocal about his opposition to the Vietnam War. Fred was seen on many newsreels, walking arm and arm with Martin Luther King Jr. One thing Jim always admired about Fred, he had the courage of his convictions. After all, Fred came from a military family. His father had even been welterweight champ of the United States Army back in the 1940s, but this background was not going to influence Fred. He was basically a rebel, but usually a rebel with a cause! Six months after Jim's birthday, Fred and Jim met for breakfast in Howard Beach.

Fred had retired from the Protection Services, Adult Department of New York State and through investments, had become extremely wealthy, which Jim felt was somewhat of a contradiction considering Fred's disdain for money, and then Fred confided in Jim that he still thought of himself as a communist. Jim instinctively replied, "Yeah! The world's richest communist."

Fred was indeed complex. He then stunned Jim again by saying he actually voted for W. Bush and thought his policies on terrorism after 9/11 had kept Americans safe and furthermore, he was very skeptical of our new president. Jim thought to himself, Fred was a communist with money that voted for Bush. How much more complex and entertaining could you get? Fred was consistent in one area—he was never dull. Jim then wondered if Fred had kept his pilot's license and if he could still fly. Wouldn't that be a kick, left-wing Fred supplying or at least piloting the plane for an assault on Bin Laden? Fred called Jim almost every week and they had both vowed not to lose touch again. During one of these phone conversations, Jim asked Fred to meet him for breakfast at a diner in Howard Beach. Howard Beach was almost the halfway mark between Jim's house in Oceanside and Fred's house in Brooklyn. As they ordered breakfast, Jim asked Fred if he still had his pilot's license, to which Fred replied, "Of course! I will not give that up until maybe they tell me I have to."

Jim thought for a moment, then asked Fred if he thought he could still pilot a small jet. Fred looked at Jim and asked why the sudden interest in his ability to fly? Jim kiddingly replied he was thinking of opening up a shuttle service for seniors.

"Where's the destination? Heaven?" They both laughed, and

Fred, knowing Jim for over fifty years, asked, "There's something deeper going on here. You want to share it with me?"

"Well, Fred, you might laugh, but this idea is worthy of you."

"What's that?" Fred now almost demanded to know.

"Look, pal," Jim said. "Remember when we were kids, you had a million schemes and I had a few ideas. You used to say your schemes were possible, but my ideas were nothing more than fantasies."

"Well!" Fred said. "What is your fantasy of the moment?"

"Hold onto your seat, my friend. A few of my friends and I think we can get Bin Laden!"

"What is this, a joke? Or wait a minute," Fred said. "I want to look around."

"Why do you want to look around?" Jim asked.

"To see if we are on *Candid Camera*, but I don't see anybody filming," Fred observed, then laughed.

"How about," Jim replied, "that I mean it."

"Then this is worse than I thought. You're insane!" Fred said. "And I know your powers of persuasion. So if you do mean it, I'm giving up my pilot's license immediately, if not sooner."

Jim looked at Fred straight in the eye and asked, "Did you or did you not say to me just recently that you were sick of America getting kicked in the ass? I think, Fred, as you're aging, you are moving more to the center."

Fred said, "Let me speak now. I agree with almost everything you said. However, I just remarried, am basically still on my honeymoon. Grace, my wife, takes care of me like I'm an only child and most important of all reasons, you're nuts! And I want to enjoy my last few years."

"I'm happy for you, Fred, but I remembered a sad story you told me at my sixty-fifth birthday that you lost a nephew 9/11. That he actually jumped from one of the towers rather than burn to death. And then you said if you had the opportunity to choke that monster with your own hands, you would do it."

Fred agreed. Yes, he had said that, but he was sure many people said crazy things like that.

"That may be true, Fred, but you always had the courage of

your conviction and I do not think that has changed, has it? My left-wing moving towards the middle friend? I am not offering you the opportunity to choke him, but at least I'm giving you the chance to kill him." Jim then stopped himself. He mustn't oversell. He was sure he had at least given Fred, as they say, food for thought.

Fred all of a sudden sat there in stunned silence. Then he broke the silence and said, "Look, even if I said yes to this preposterous plan—whatever it is and God only knows what you're capable of cooking up!—do you even know where he is?"

"Fred, here's something for you to chew on," Jim uttered in his softest voice because some people at the other tables seemed to be eavesdropping. "What if by some stroke of fate I do know, or at least have a good idea, as to where he is? Would you at least consider it?"

"Jim! If I thought there was a better than fifty-fifty chance that you knew where he was, yes, I would have to consider it. In the meantime, wet my appetite—you wouldn't have gone this far unless you think you know something!" Fred sat back and waited for Jim to reply. This ought to be good, he thought to himself.

Jim leaned forward and whispered to Fred, "Let's go out to the car. There are too many eyes and ears in here and they are getting a floorshow. "

Fred and Jim both got into Jim's car. Jim continued where he left off in the diner.

"Listen closely, Trotsky. You will be the only one to know what I know after I tell you what inspired this whole plan. While my wife Lynn was recuperating from her recent surgeries, I got in the habit of going every morning to Delightful Doughnuts for coffee. One morning, I bumped into a friend there who told me that the owner of this doughnut shop had just moved next door to his sister. And one day while he was doing some work on his sister's house, this guy came over and introduced himself. He also tells me this guy is Pakistani and owns thirty-three dough-nut shops."

Fred interrupts Jim and asks, "What has this got to do with

Bin Laden?"

"Gorby!" Jim says. "Just listen. While my friend and I are discussing the economy, this medium-sized, fortyish guy comes strolling over to our table. He says hello to my friend and my friend introduces me to Ayub saying, 'Jim, this is the guy I was just telling you about.' We exchange greetings and this Ayub then walks to his office in the back of the doughnut shop."

Fred again interrupts Jim and says, "Okay! So far you told me you met a medium-sized, fortyish Pakistani guy that owns thirty-three doughnut shops! This better get a lot more interesting because so far the only thing you succeeded in doing is giving me an urge for a doughnut and when you're a diabetic like me, that ain't good."

Jim then says, "Fidel! I am not finished yet, give me a chance!"

Fred, a little agitated, says, "I'll give you a chance, but quit calling me those commie names or you better start taking flying lessons."

"Don't be so thin-skinned," Jim shoots back. "I'll get down to the meat. This Ayub, after seeing me three or four times at the doughnut shop, decides to befriend me. We start talking first about small stuff, but with each subsequent meeting, the conversations get a little deeper. I compliment him and tell him he sounds like he was born in Brooklyn, not Pakistan."

Fred again interrupts and says, "Only you would think that's a compliment."

"Well!" Jim says. "You know what I meant. He had only a very slight accent, but anyway, I now start asking him questions about Pakistan and he's readily giving me answers. He tells me things like Pakistan is the sixth most populous country in the world and five percent of the people control the wealth and it is the only country whose people are getting shorter with each generation mainly because of their lack of nutrition."

Fred, losing his patience, says, "So far you told me about doughnut shops, short Pakistanis that are getting shorter with time and," Fred observes, "if that's the case, in a thousand years, they might just disappear."

"All right, Fred, cut the comedy!" Jim says. "I'm getting to the good part. This Ayub tells me his family is part of the five percent that rule the country."

"Let me guess," Fred says. "He offered you a doughnut franchise in Pakistan."

"You want to get serious?" Jim replied. "Ayub's brother is head of the I.S.I."

"Explain I.S.I.," Fred asks.

"As explained to me by Ayub, the I.S.I. is equivalent to the American C.I.A. and is totally responsible for all security in Pakistan. They know everything that goes on in that area of the world."

"Yeah!" Fred says. "How do you know this guy is not blowing smoke rings? How do you know what he's telling you is even fifty percent true?"

"I don't know," Jim said, "but when I ask him if his brother knows where Bin Laden is, he says, 'of course, and so does your government'. Yeah! I ask Ayub, 'where is he'? Ayub then tells me he loves America and is very active in American politics. Get this, Ayub tells me he's a Republican and proceeds to show me snapshots with all the leading Republicans in New York."

Fred asks, "Jim, get back to the meat. Did he ever tell you where Bin Laden is?"

Jim tells Fred, "Yes." He takes out some notes from his pocket and starts reading, then stops and says, "Fred, he also said our government for some cockeyed reason did not want him killed."

"Where is he?" Fred was growing impatient.

Jim went back to his notes and told Fred, "Bin Laden is in Pakistan right outside of Jalalabad, right by the Khyber pass at a Paki military base, where he has been for seven years."

"You mean he operates out of there?"

"No! Fred, according to Ayub's brother, Bin Laden is under lock and key and he's more like a prisoner and there's a rich Saudi family that's paying the Pakistani military large sums of money to keep him alive."

"Jim," Fred says, "you have indeed gotten my interest. I am going to digest what you have told me and call some ex-disenchanted military people I know and see if there is any validity in what you have been told."

"If you do that," Jim quipped, "You might raise some, pardon the expression, 'red flags.'"

"Who is being funny now?" Fred laughs, and says, "You always tell me how smart I was. Believe me, I'm not going to give anything away."

"You do that," Jim said. "And I'll go back to Stoney and see if I can pump him some more."

Fred looks at Jim and says, "Who the hell is Stoney?"

"That's right, I forgot to tell you." Jim smiles and tells Fred, "Ayub wanted so bad to be an American. He decided to take a nickname."

"Where did he come up with Stoney?" Fred asked.

Jim smiled and told Fred, "Ayub really wanted to be called Rocky, but there were too many Rockys in New York. Thus, the nickname's Stoney."

Fred said, "Okay, I heard enough." He gets out of the car and leaves. Jim returns home, got on the phone, called the guys and asked them to get to the diner a little earlier than usual Saturday morning.

14. PLUS TWO IS EIGHT

The guys were early that Saturday as Jim requested. This time, Jim had requested a table in the private room usually reserved for showers and birthday parties. Jim was feeling more and more confident each day, especially since Fred had called him and to his amazement, said he was interested. Fred's snooping around some of his ex-military friends seemed to have substantiated a lot of what Jim told him. In Fred's words, "Everything you told me, I've been told is quite possible."

Jim asked Fred, "What about your honeymoon?" to which Fred winked at Jim and stated, "Hey! This honeymoon has already lasted longer than two of my marriages."

Armed with the knowledge that his buddy Fred aboard, Jim could now expand on his plan. He addressed the guys and asked if anyone had cold feet. He asked them to speak up now.

Phil was the first to speak, saying, "My feet are always cold and when that happens, I have to piss." He excused himself and said he would be right back.

Jim then looked at the rest of the guys. "Tom, Dom, Steve, Bill, are you guys still all right with this?"

Nods of yes came from all around the table. Phil came back and the meeting started. Jim gave them the workout schedule he had arranged with Nelson, informed them of the cover story and suggested that they start laying the groundwork on the baseball touring story. Tom commented that he thought it was a perfect cover.

"Since we have been talking about doing this for the last three years," Tom said.

Steve grumpily said, "I don't have to give stories to anybody."

Jim reminded him if his wife Sabina was still alive, he might reconsider that thought.

Steve yells, "You wanna bet!"

Jim says, "Steve is right. Sabina knew better than to ask questions about his line of work."

"What line of work is that?"

The table grew silent, then everyone laughed. Jim then told the guys there was something else on the agenda.

"What is that?" asked Dom. "Are we going to the assisted living homes to recruit more people?"

"No," said Jim, "but there has been a recruitment! And I hope there will be no objections."

Just then on cue, Nelse and Fred walked in. All the guys knew Nelson through Jim and liked him, but Fred was new to them. Jim gave them Fred's background, carefully omitting the communist part. Then he asked Fred and Nelson to leave the room and wait in the lobby. Jim then explained to the guys that they needed Fred—he was smart and more importantly, he was a licensed pilot and a navigator. And Nelson just seemed to want to be a part of something exciting.

"If there are any objections, let's hear them now!"

Billy was the first to speak, saying, "I never knew there were so many guys that were tired of living."

"If they're serious," Tom said, "the more the merrier."

Phil curiously seemed a little pissed. He said, "That's it. No one else!"

Steve put in his dime's worth. "You know the more people, the more chance of this failing."

Dom wanted to know how Jim talked all these people into maybe throwing away their lives. Jim looks at Dom and says, "Is that a compliment or an indictment?" and then asked the guys if it was okay to ask Nelson and Fred back to the table. Collectively, the guys say, "Bring them in." Jim welcomes the new recruits and tells them that the guys are glad to have them on board!

Jim then looks at the guys and says, "Okay, guys! Hands on

the table palms down!"

Jim then guided Fred and Nelson's hands to the table and they whispered, "Bonus time."

The Senior Six were now the Senior Eight. In parting, Jim reminded the guys that he would see them at the gym the following Monday at 8am and to make sure Nelson had their medical histories and all the medications they were on. He then added that, now that the plan was getting serious, their regular meetings would be stepped up to three times a week.

"P.S.," Jim said. "The gym classes will be private. However, at the gym there will be no mention of our plan. Next when we meet, I will give out the assignments to each of you and Phil, since you live alone. I suggest all future meetings to be held at your house. We will put your table next to the john so you will not have far to walk."

15. THE RETURN

Jim returned to Delightful Doughnuts for his coffee and a doughnut almost every morning. The third morning of the week, Stoney came in, spotted Jim and came over to the table. Both men started shooting the breeze about baseball, the weather and politics. Stoney was feeling good as the man he backed, considered a long shot, was elected Nassau County Executive and Stoney was thinking of giving him a party in one of his doughnut shops. Jim then asked Stoney if he could ever consider going back to Pakistan to live. Stoney immediately and adamantly replied, "Never! This is my country now!"

Pakistan, he said, thought to be a democracy by the rest of the world, to him was considered more of a dictatorship that was run by generals and a puppet president. Jim figured now that he had Stoney started on the politics of his home country, he would hit Stoney with a series of probing questions. The first of which was did he think that Pakistan was a staunch ally of the United States? Stoney again replied quickly and adamantly.

"Yes!" he said. "Until the money runs out."

Jim asked Stoney to elaborate.

"Easy," he said. "As long as Bin Laden is on the loose, America will continue to send billions of dollars to Pakistan to buy their support. If and when Bin Laden is found, that money will immediately dry up and that would cause misery to the generals and other selective people who have been lining their own pockets. The rich Saudis and the American government would turn off the faucet, creating a free-for-all in the Pakistani government."

"What you are telling me, Stoney, for now at least, is that he remains under lock and key at that military base in Pakistan?"

Stoney looks at Jim and asks, "Are you some type of secret agent? Or as they now call them, a spook?"

Jim looked at Stoney. "Do you think I'm—what is that you said? Oh, yes! A spook?"

Stoney shot back, "Not really. You're too damn old!"

They both laughed and Stoney asked Jim if one day he would join him at his gold club in Brookville. Jim said yes and gave him his cell phone number and then they both went about their business.

As Jim got back in his car, he reflected on his conversation with Stoney and now was convinced Stoney knew what he was talking about. Jim then thought about Fred who, in the beginning at least, wanted no part of Jim's plan. What thing that Jim hit upon changed his mind? He felt Fred made a rather quick one-hundred-and-eighty degree turn. Jim then remembered even as kids when something rang his bell, he went ahead one-hundred-and-twenty percent and no one could ever change his mind.

16. THE ASSIGNMENTS

The following Saturday, the first meeting at Phil's place was underway. All eight guys sat around Phil's dining room table. Jim pointed out to the guys that they were getting closer. Right away the comedy started. Bill led it off with, "Yeah, we are all getting closer to a heart attack! Nelson is killing us." Jim remarked he was already down 5 lbs. calling himself the incredible shrinking man!

"'Boot Camp for Seniors' my ass," Dom said. "I think Nelson here has a deal with the local cemeteries."

Jim cut them short and said, "Let's get back to reality."

"Reality!" Tom said. "I like it better in this fantasy world you put is all in."

Jim felt the guys were ready for some more information. "Gentlemen, there is an eighty percent chance that I know where Bin Laden is and why."

"How about sharing that with us, Sherlock?" Dom quipped.

"I do not think at this time the timing is right. The less people that know, the better. But I promise you," Jim said, "as we get closer, all of us will know exactly what I know and no wise comments please. As you guys can see, in front of you is a pad and pencil. Use them to write down your assignments, then memorize them and then burn the paper they are written on."

This, of course, drew a comment from Steve, who said, "After we burn these papers, are we all made men?"

"Yeah, made in America," Jim replied. "And coincidentally, wasn't it the made men the mafia that during World War II made the invasion of Sicily easier? We digress," Jim said, "but let's start with you, Steve. Arrange through your relatives, friends or whatever they're referred to these days as for a leased jet to be located in Catania, Sicily."

"Why in Catania?" Steve said.

Jim then told the guys the reason was that Catania was exactly 2860 miles in a straight line to Paki-Afghan border.

"So what you're saying," Bill blurted out, "is that the butcher is in Pakistan."

"Maybe," Jim replied, and continued, "Bill, you give Steve all the help he needs. After all, you speak Italian fluently. And Dom, you call all the guys at home and make sure you mention to anyone that answers the phone—and in most cases, it's the wives—make sure you plant the seeds about the baseball trip. Be enthusiastic and extremely sincere. Fred, you know your assignment. Hone your flying skills, read up on small jet passenger planes, check navigation routes between Catania and the Paki-Afghan border. Phil, you stay close to me and be liaison between me and the guys and when there's a meeting or an agenda change, you will notify all the guys individually. Nelson, your job, of course, is to evaluate everyone and get us in reasonable shape without killing us. Tom, I would like you to research everything about explosives. We have to know what is literally going to give us the biggest bang for our buck."

Dom interrupts and asks, "Jim, what is your job?"

"My job," Jim replies, "is to get the money to finance this mission!" And then he announces, "The meeting is over. Let's hear a big 'bonus time'!"

And then they leave.

17. THE FINANCE

Jim left the meeting somewhat sad. Perhaps it was because of the sound of his own words that kept echoing in his head—'It's my job to get the financing.' How? Where? How much? The enormity of the whole mission finally hit him squarely between the eyes. Up until now, everything fell into place. It was enough to ask the guys to probably give up their lives, now he couldn't ask them to finance the plan! That had a good chance of killing them. As patriotic as they were, they definitely would not hurt the security of their families. Just then, a light went off in Jim's head. He remembered two pages that appeared in *Newsday* right about 9/11. They listed all the companies in the Towers that lost people. At the top was a brokerage house called Bantor Herald that had lost over one-hundred people. Jim also knew at least three people that still held rather big jobs with them. If he could find a way to get to the CEO of that company, maybe he could come up with the financing. Didn't that CEO vow that no matter what, whether it took money or otherwise, he would make sure all the families would be taken care of? He also stated that he wouldn't rest until the murderer Bin Laden was put to rest. Then, Jim thought, even if he was to get to this guy, he would have to reveal too much and what if this CEO thinks Jim is crazy and reports him? Jim thought, this guy spoke with such courage and conviction then, but would that passion still be with him after many years had passed and a lot of politics had been played with 9/11? If Jim gets that far as to see this CEO, would he be capable of making the sales pitch of his life? There could be no fumbles, no errors, no misrepresentations or else the whole plan is dead. Did he want to risk that? Then another thought had occurred to Jim. He didn't stop to figure out how much financing he would need. He was beginning to feel overwhelmed. This step was going to be extremely delicate. Jim felt a pounding in his head compounded by the ringing of his cellphone. It was Fred!

"I checked around with some ex-military people that used to be in the know— and I stress the words 'used to be.' I told them I was doing some research for a book I might write about Bin Laden. When I got to asking them if they thought Bin Laden was being protected by the Pakistani military, they answered that it was very possible. When I asked them if they thought he was at a Pakistani military base near Western Afghanistan, they clammed up and gave me eerie stares. I think we are on to something." Fred continued, "And if I was a betting man—and I am—I would bet the butcher is there and your information is correct."

Jim agreed and Fred sensed something in Jim's voice was not right. Fred asked, "Are we still going to do this thing?"

"Fred, we have to talk," Jim replied. "You know, I think you are one of the brightest guys I know. I have to run some things by you and not on the phone."

Jim and Fred met at the Canarsie Pier in Brooklyn.

Fred asks Jim, "What has got you down, buddy?"

"The enormity of this whole thing is weighing me down," Jim responds.

"I believe you mean the financing," Fred observed.

"You are right, but I do have some ideas I'd like to run by you." Jim tells Fred about the Banter Merrill and says that could be a good place to start raising money.

Fred looks at Jim and screams, "Are you fucking crazy? The next thing I know, you'll be asking newspapers and telling them of your plan!"

"Look!" Jim said. "I know it sounds crazy, but what am I supposed to do, go to my local banker and ask for a loan to kill Bin Laden?"

"No," Fred answered, "ask me! I've already thought about it

and I figure it will take roughly two million dollars. Didn't you tell me that I am the richest communist this side of Putin? Yes! Your friend moving towards the center Fred will put up the money. You know I think money makes you weak! Furthermore, I'm not going to let you go to those fat cat Wall Streeters that would sell their mothers if there was a profit in it."

"Are you sure, Fred?" Jim asked.

"Don't worry, buddy, I'm sure!"

"Fred, I would like to ask you a question. What turned you around on this whole thing?"

"I wasn't going to tell you this, but after you told me about the plan, I was all set to find a reason to turn you down," Fred said. "The following day, I had a doctor's appointment and he informed me that my heart had gotten worse and the new valve was leaking. Perhaps, he said, if I was lucky, I had a year."

Jim just sat there. "Then," he thought out loud, "they probably all had just a year exactly!"

Fred said, "Why not go out at least trying to do something you believe in?"

18. THE NEW PRESIDENT

The new American president continued on his tour of the countries, apologizing and redefining the personality of America. He bowed to world leaders, trying to convince them that despite all the venom that has been directed at the United States, America still respected them. The rogue nations of the world took his actions to be a sign of weakness and laughed amongst themselves while still making plans to finance terrorism all over the world. Many Americans perceived the new president to be a socialist—even Fred the communist thought that. Tea Parties began to spring up everywhere and a backlash was building strength, especially among older Americans who were already feeling alienated.

19. STEVE THE AMBASSADOR

Steve continued to meet with people from all over when he realized that he had family in Sicily who were very well connected on both sides of the fence. He would have to make a trip to Sicily, which wouldn't be such a bad idea since he would again get to see his cousin once removed! A curious expression, Steve thought. Once removed from what? Lucia was a beautiful woman eighteen years Steve's junior. During his rare visits to the island, Steve has grown very fond of her and thought the feeling was mutual, but surely, he figured, she must be married by now and after all, she was family. Steve called Billy and asked if he thought he could get away for a week. He needed him to accompany him to Sicily for no longer than a week.

"I'll work it out," Billy replied. "You handle the details, I'll be there."

Billy knew why Steve needed him. He was fluent in Italian and although Steve spoke the language, he very often fractured it and what they needed had to be fully understood by all parties. The only problem, Steve thought, was Billy looked so much like a cop. He even had cop hair. But then he remembered Sicily's history. Just about everyone had invaded that little island and from the beginning, the Arabs were there, followed by the Greeks, then the French and even the Vikings—and let's not forget the Italians. That's why they always said Sicilians come in many colors, Steve thought, even in his family. He had blond, green-eyed relatives as well as very dark-skinned relatives with black hair, so maybe Billy wouldn't be a problem as long as he was not redheaded. Some Sicilians even today feel redheads are bad luck. Why? Because folklore told them that Judas was a redhead.

20. LET'S PLAY BALL

Dom was busy making repetitive calls to all the guys homes, hoping their wives would pick up the phone and in most cases, they did. This way he could plant the baseball seeds about the upcoming tour, which he did, showing great enthusiasm about the upcoming trip in April or May. While making one of these phone calls, Dom began getting terrible pains in his chest. He got in his car and drove to the emergency room at St. Francis Hospital in Manhasset. In the emergency room, he filled in the ER on all the surgeries he had. They then asked him what medicines he was on. Dom replied, "Too many to remember," but then Jim's words came to mind: "Make a list of all the medicines you take and make sure Nelson gets a copy." Dom reached into his pocket and pulled out of his wallet the list of medicines he was on. The ER was impressed and congratulated Dom on being so well prepared and then they rolled him off for a series of tests.

21. THE BIG BANG THEORY

Tommy was becoming a maven on explosives. He bought every book he could get his hands on. He tried to be careful not to arouse any suspicions while he was making these purchases. Although Tommy was extremely high strung and even when he was an altar boy serving mass he always looked like he was up to something. Tommy reasoned that purchasing the books wouldn't arouse too much interest, but if he went to the library, he feared it might raise eyebrows. If he checked a book out or asked for information about books on explosives, those old biddies in the library were helpful, but also very nosy, and Tom was cautious and sometimes paranoid. His reasoning was good, though! He thought some kid at the checkout wouldn't care what he was purchasing.

Phil called Jim and said, "You asked me to stay close. What is going on?"

Jim told Phil to visit all the guys personally and from this point on, no phone calls! Jim told Phil, "Inform the guys. It's important that they report the progress on their assignments. Tell them we meet at 9 a.m. at your house Saturday."

Phil said, "I got to go."

"Wait!" Jim said.

"I can't," Phil said. "When I got to go, I got to go. See you Saturday."

Saturday rolled around and the guys were all seated around Phil's dining room table, which luckily for Phil was only ten feet away from his bathroom. Jim asked Steve to start things off.

Steve said he was optimistic and that he already had made contact with relatives in Sicily and he and Bill would be going there to make sure they understand exactly what kind of plan they need. Billy's expertise in Italian should insure there would be no misunderstandings.

Bill chimed in with, "All the arrangements are made. We leave tomorrow and should be gone less than a week."

Dom's turn came and he told the guys what they already knew—that he had already called each house twice and discussed the baseball tour at length and he was getting so excited, he forgot the whole story was just a cover. In some cases, the wives started asking questions.

"And in one case, your wife, Jim, asked why the women couldn't go!" Dom said. "She said, 'While the guys are at the ballgames, the women could go shopping.' But I told her it was a guys only trip."

Jim then asked Tom how his journey into the world of explosives was doing.

Tom said, "I have identified the explosives! The purchase and then the transportation to Catania will be the hard part. I will definitely be more specific at our next meeting, but I will tell you guys this—America is a great country. You can get a book on almost anything! Imagine, any crazy bastard could not only find out where to purchase explosives, but if they wanted to be creative and make a bomb, they could find out how to do that!"

Nelson looked at the guys and remarked, "It is amazing! Almost as amazing as the shape I'm trying to get these guys into. But all kidding aside, they are working very hard at it." Nelson then asks Dom, "Are you still getting chest pains?"

Dom doesn't say anything, he just looks at Jim. Jim breaks the silence and asks, "Dom, what about the chest pains?"

Dom looks at Nelson and says, "Nelson, you got a big mouth." Dom then tells the guys what happened and that he's waiting for the results of all the tests they gave him at St. Francis, but it has since passed and he feels great—until Nelson's Death Camp for Seniors!

"You mean Boot Camp!" Nelson says.

"No, I mean Death Camp," Dom reiterates.

All the guys laugh.

Fred then reports that he is brushing up on his flying and the trick as he sees it is how will the guys will fly undetected from Sicily to Pakistan? The direct route would normally take them over four countries one of them being Iran which isn't exactly friendly airspace. This was a big hitch, Fred knew, and he asked for more time to figure it out.

Jim then calls the meeting to a close. But before he does he says something that jars the others to immediate silence. "We're getting close," he says "It's time to get your wills in order.

The meeting ends. The guys start to file out of Phil's house. Jim calls them back for a "Bonus time!" Then when the guys start to leave, Jim asks Dom to stay behind with he and Phil. Jim asks Phil if he's going to be all right. Phil assures Jim there isn't any problem other than his frequent peeing and not to get any ideas because he was definitely going!

"Yeah," Jim said. "You're definitely going too much!"

"Very funny," Phil replies and then says, "I think you should be more worried about Dom here."

"That's my next question. How are you feeling, Dom?"

"With my hands," Dom sarcastically replies.

Jim tells Dom to sit out the rest of Nelson's classes, then he thinks to himself, "Maybe we ought to shut down the classes for all of us. We don't want anybody dropping dead of a heart attack." He calls Nelson the next day and Nelson convinces Jim that the guys should at least do some light cardio work. Jim tells Nelson, "Everyone but Dom and Fred," and asks Nelson not to question him.

22. "ARE YOU KIDDING ME"?

C.I.A. director Lon Beletta sat at his desk wondering what his two field agents had to tell him that was so important. At exactly 1 pm, his two agents were ushered into his office. They looked at there boss, and they younger of the two, Mike Dee, started t talk. "Some information has come to us that there are some crazy old coots that have this idea that they can take out Bin Laden". Beletta's face lit up with an ear to ear grin. The second field agent Scott Davis, added, "Sir, they claim to know exactly where he is". "Yeah", Beletta says, "Where's that?". "They claim he is at or near a military base in Pakistan, near the Afghan border. They also say he is being protected by the Pakistani military". Beletta's grin turned to a cold stare. He looked at his men and told them he wanted these old men identified and followed 24 hours a day. Beletta then asked his agents, "How accurate is this information, and where did it come from?". Mike Dee replied, "It came from some retired military officer, who claimed he had been contacted by an old Air Force pal of his who needed him to very information regarding the location of Bin Laden". "How high up on the chain was this retired military officer?", asked Beletta. "A retired captain from Military Air Transport?, Davis answered, "Which by the way, was the same group as the guy who had asked him the question". "Who was this guy asking these questions?", Beletta asked. "His name is Fred Santos" answered Mike Dee, "Both he an our informant, ex-captain Tom Maher were asshole buddies who even years ago were considered a bit radical. Maher seems to have reformed with his old age, but Santos seems still to have maintained his radical ways". Beletta dismissed his two agents and immediately notified the President that a group of crazy old men had somehow figured out the location of Bin Laden. This location of course, had been known by the President, the C.I.A., and the joint chiefs of staff for over two years. An elite group of fighters were now being trained in Afghanistan to take Bin Laden out. The President was waiting for the perfect opportunity to strike to present itself. He knew he was being perceived as soft and naïve. His popularity was waning as fast as the gas prices were escalating. He ordered C.I.A. director Beletta, "make sure nothing gets in the way of our ultimate mission". Beletta himself knew, they they could not afford under any circumstances, to tip off the Pakistan military that they had Bin Laden in their sights. "These old guys", Beletta thought, "Were unknowingly getting in the way".

23. THE FAMILY VISIT

Steve and Billy arrive in Catania and are met by the beautiful Lucia. Steve looks at her and thinks that time has been good to her. She was as attractive as he remembered. Steve right away wondered if she had ever married. Lucia and Billy engage in conversation, chattering away in Italian. Then Lucia turns to Steve and in broken English says, "Cuisine, your friend speaks Italian well for an American!"

Steve answers, "That's why he's here."

Lucia then tells Steve she was very sorry to hear of his wife's passing.

"Yes!" Steve says. "She was a wonderful person."

Lucia then tells Steve that she lost her husband, Pino, at about the same time. "However," she continued, "let us talk about happier things! We have a feast planned for you and your friend at my brother Marco's villa in Taoromina."

"Your brother Marco has done well! His reputation has reached the shores of America," Steve replied.

When Steve looked at Lucia his heart pounded. He could not get over her raw beauty. Steve also felt a certain surge to his libido he hadn't felt in years. The Sicilians had an expression for this feeling. Loosely translated it meant hit by a lightening bolt.

"Beyond well!" Lucia said. "He is one of the most respected men in all of Italy and you know it's a Sicilian custom to grant a wish to a relative that returns to the island, so prepare yourself!"

Billy remarks, "Believe me, he is prepared."

Steve shoots a glance at Billy and Billy shuts up for the rest of the ride.

As Lucia pulls up to cousin Marco's villa, they are greeted by a throng of relatives. Steve is somewhat bewildered. He knew he had relatives in Sicily, but he hadn't any idea that he had this many!

The festivities continued until sun came up. But after the last guest left, Steve was summoned to a large room with a 12 foot ceiling and two large heavy oak doors that would close gently behind him. He walked toward the middle where Marco was seated and sipping a Sambuca. Marco put his glass down, gave Steve a hug and in pure Sicilian told Steve how happy he was to have Steve in his home. Steve in his choppy Italian thanked Marco and then said he had a big favor to ask of him but first he wanted to know if his friend Billy could join them because he was fluent in all dialects of Italian. Marco, who had met Billy earlier, was surprised.

"Your friend Bill does not look Italian." Marco said.

Steve replied, "He is not, at least by blood. He's Greek."

Marco laughs and says "Half of Sicily is Greek."

Marco then summons one of his men to have him bring Steve's friend Billy to the room.

Billy enters the room, feeling somewhat intimidated., not just by the size of the room but by the way he was escorted in. He asked Steve if he is expected to bow or kiss Marco's ring.

"No, my friend," Steve says, "Just stand here, be cordial and make sure everyone understands what's being said. We can't afford any fuck-ups."

Marco evidently understands the term "fuck-ups" and asks "What do you mean fuck-up?"

Steve pulls Billy closer to him and Marco.

"I'm going to speak English," Steve says to Billy, "You must translate to my cousin. No shortcuts, no fuck-ups!"

Again, but this time in Sicilian Marco says "Che cosa fuck-ups?"

Steve says "Cugino, I have a huge favor to ask of you. You

are a very respected man throughout Europe and the Middle East and it is well known that you have built many successful businesses throughout Italy. You are a legend among the poor, the rich, the political world and the underworld. "

Marco waits for Billy to end his translation and then says "What am I Caesar? You came here to praise me?"

Steve replies, "Cugino, I and my friends need your help. We need an 8 passenger jet plane to be ready for us at the Catania Fontanarossa airport."

After Billy translates, Steve looks at Marco's face for some kind of expression but there was none. Marco then replied that he was disappointed. He thought Steve had come back to see his family. But now he finds the only reason for Steve's visit is because Steve needs his help. Steve found it curious that Marco hadn't yet asked him why he needs the plane. Marco looks at Steve and says in Italian "I'm waiting."

Steve shoots back "For what?!"

Marco says to Steve "Do you think I was made with a finger? You will not receive any help from me unless you tell me what you and your friends are planning. If it does not bring any harm to my country and my people, I might consider it."

Steve had to make a quick decision. He decided if they were ever going to get this plane, he had to tell Marco everything; something Steve wasn't used to doing.

Billy translated as Marco listened intently. Selling was never Steve's strong suit. In fact, most of the time when he spoke, he had a way of irritating people. Bill, recognizing this, was able to soften the translation. When Billy was done, Marco gave Steve a penetrating stare.

Marco finally spoke "You have balls my cousin. If I supply you with a plane so that you can carry out this operation, I automatically become an accessory. Why should I put myself in that position?"

Steve replied, "You are a businessman and I can make it worth your while."

"Americans think everything can be taken care of with money," Marco replied.

Steve barked back "Fuck you Marco, you didn't lose anyone in those burning towers. Almost all of my guys did. Money is not the issue with us," Steve continued.

Marco, taken by his cousin's tone and the tears in his eyes, waited for Billy to translate and then replied.

"I see you have inherited the hot blood of your family and for your information, I have lost a Godson to terrorism. It was domestic terrorism. In 1988, my Godson was kidnapped by the Red Brigade. I was unable to save him. Leftist terrorists killed him in cold blood. They also assassinated my best friend because of his political views. So I have been touched by terrorism and that is why I am going to help you. Are you surprised, Cugino?"

Billy and Steve looked at each other. From Marco's tone, that's not the answer they were expecting. But Marco wasn't through surprising them.

Marco then reiterated Americans think money buys everything and with a sly smile, he continued.

"They are right." Marco says.

And so came the business end of the deal. Marco wanted $500,000 American dollars for himself and $250,000 for the lease of the plane. Steve thought all is right with the world. With money you get honey. He preferred it that way. This was the world he was brought up in. The two words he understood best were the two "Ms," money and murder.

Steve finally spoke and Billy translated.

"Those arrangements will work, Cugino."

Marco then turned back into being a host and offered the two men a nightcap.

Marco summoned his sister, Lucia and asked her to show Billy and Steve to their rooms. Then good-naturedly added "I'm sure Lucia would like to tuck her cousin Steve in." Marco then began to laugh so hard, he almost choked on his nightcap. Billy laughed and Steve shot him a piercing look.

24. "THESE GUYS ARE SERIOUS"

Beletta is not believing what he is hearing from his field people. "This is unbelievable", he thinks to himself. "How did these antiques get even this far? Now they have gone to Sicily! What are they trying to accomplish there?" Mike Dee interrupts, "You know Mr. Director, Sicily is in a direct line with Pakistan, maybe that is where they are going to launch their attack from?". Beletta blurts out, "Are these guys that smart? This would be funny if it weren't so serious." Mike Dee suggested that they could all be brought in for questioning, but it was vetoed by Beletta who said, "That's the last thing we need. We cannot bring attention to what we have to do. I want each one of them followed closely, this thing cannot blow up in our face. We are so close, we cannot fuck up now!".

25. An Explosive Situation

Tommy sat there thinking that the guys are going to be amazed to hear that in America, if you want to build a bomb, there's a book that tells you exactly how to do it. If you're shopping for explosives, there are books to tell you where you can readily get your hands on them. Tom glowed with satisfaction knowing that he was able to find exactly what they needed. The only obstacle Tom saw was getting the explosives to Sicily.

Jim called Phil and told him to arrange a meeting as soon as Bill and Steve returned to New York on Tuesday. Phil would then arrange for all the guys to meet at his house on Wednesday. Since Phil was divorced and no one was ever around, his house auomatically became home base for all the "secret" meetings.

Wednesday came around very quickly. As the guys gathered, they remarked how well Steve and Billy looked upon returning from Italy. First business to get to was the news Steve and Billy had brought home with them.

"The result is my cousin has agreed to help us! The plane isn't a problem, he will handle that. The plane—whichever one we decide on—will be at the Catania Airport. We must let him know one week in advance. The plane will be leased, a small passenger, fully fueled jet of the type we request. And last but not least, he wants $500,000 for him and $250,000 for a one week lease of the plane, as long as it is a small passenger jet like a Dassault Falcon 7X or a Lear Jet 35A—both are the same size. The Lear seats eight and cruises at 529 miles per hour. The Dessault Falcon cruises at 580 miles per hour. Both have the same seating and relatively the same range, around 6500 miles. Cousin Marco suggests the Falcon, but he realizes that the decision on the plane would have to be made by whoever pilots the plane and the degree of comfort he has with the plane he chooses. My cousin also promised there would be no questions asked at the airport. A flight plan would be filed by one of his people."

Jim congratulated Steve and Billy on a fine job, even though to himself he was thinking the price is very steep. Next up was Tom. Everyone to a man was still trying to digest what Steve had said—the $750,000 apparently stuck in everybody's throat. Jim, reading the situation, said, "Listen, guys. You didn't expect this guy to help us just because he is Steve's cousin! There is a reason he is who he is."

"Yeah!" Dom says. "A fuckin' thief!"

Steve takes exception to Dom's remark. "What do you think we are dealing with, choir boys?"

"I know," Tom says. "Can I give my report now?"

"Certainly," Jim says. "Go ahead!"

Tom tells the guys that the explosive they needed was called semtex. "It's main component is Pet-N and its plasticized by the incorporation of Styrene Butadiene Copylimer."

Jim interrupts Tommy and says, "English, Tommy. Speak English."

Tom says, "Okay. Explosives were manufactured in Pardubice in the former Czech Republic. Pardubice is located one-hundred miles East of Prague. The explosives were manufactured in large quantities by a company called Synthesism. These explosives were supplied to the communists during the Vietnam War."

Bill says, "Enough with the history lesson. How and where do we get it? I also suggest we now refer to the explosives as the product."

Jim says, "Bill's right. From now on, it's the product."

Tom says, "Product! Explosive! I don't give a fuck. Can I continue without being fucking interrupted?"

"I'm sorry, Tom," Jim apologizes and asks Tom to continue.

"Where was I? Oh, yes! The product was used to supply the communists' forces during the Vietnam War. When the war ended, the Czech Republic had large quantities of the explosives. I mean, product for sale. Most of which was sold to Libya, which I might add is right on Sicily's doorstep. In turn, Libya 'til this day feeds it to the terrorists all over the world. The product is relatively cheap and just one pound of it can cause mass destruction."

Nelson wanted to know how we get it and then how do we get it to Sicily without the product being detected?

"That is easy," Tom says. "The product is stable and stores well. It's not readily detected by x-rays. The product is also malleable, very powerful and odorless and cannot even be detected by sniffing dogs and the beauty is, we only need about twenty pounds to wipe out a half-mile area. The product can be detonated in many ways, the simplest of which is with a fuse or wrapping rags around the explosive, pouring some diesel oil on the rags, lighting it and drop. We can also get very technical, such as attaching small switches, but I think that is unnecessary. As the popular cliché points out, keep it simple!"

"Excellent job, Tom!" Jim congratulates Tom, but realizes that this poses another challenge. Who do we contact in Libya? How do we contact them and how do we get the product out of Libya and to Sicily? Jim then asks Steve if he could make another trip and ask his cousin if he could help us contact the right people and then help us get the product to Sicily. Steve agrees rather quickly to go back to Sicily and see his cousin.

Billy remarks, "Which cousin are you going to see?"

Steve shoots Billy that look and Billy shuts up. Jim tries to diffuse the situation by saying, "I understand you have a kissing cousin over there!"

Steve shoots Jim a look and Jim changes the subject. Jim asks Tom if he knows how far the product in Libya is from Catania. Fred jumps in and says, "I can answer that! It's less than 450 miles from Tripoli, Libya to Catania, Sicily. Years ago," Fred continued, "before Khadafi, it was a stopover point for military air transports that I flew and navigated on many occasions."

Jim reiterated how critical Steve's next meeting with his cousin Marco is. "I'm putting a lot on your shoulders, Steve," Jim continues. "Your cousin has to help us contact these people and then help us arrange getting the product to Sicily. Do you anticipate any problems? Don't forget, we are giving your cousin $500,000 for his assistance."

"Yes," Steve said, "but now we have changed the deal! I'll do my best, but don't expect any miracles."

"If we have to," Jim says, "we will sweeten the pot $250,000, but leave that as a last resort."

"You are a very generous man with my money," Fred mutters.

Jim looks at Fred and says, "Don't you agree his cousin at this point is indispensible? And if he is as powerful as Steve says he is, that part of our troubles are over."

Fred looks at Jim and says, "Or just beginning. We are relying a lot on a man neither one of us has met."

Dom announces he has to pick up his grandchildren and asks the guys to put their hands on the table. They all yell, "Bonus time!"

The meeting breaks up and Jim asks Fred to hang back so they can discuss the finances. They decide the budget is one million for the product, possibly seven-hundred-and-fifty thousand for Steve's cousin and another two-hundred-and-fifty thousand for lease of the plane.

"And if we need more money?" Fred snorts.

"Let us cross that bridge, as Senator Kennedy used to say, when we come to it!" Jim then went on to point out that maybe Steve's cousin will be happy with the five-hundred thousand. "That would leave us an extra two-hundred-and-fifty thousand."

"Forever the optimist," Fred replies.

Seven days later, Steve returns from Sicily. Phil contacts all the guys for a meeting at his house per Jim's request. Steve, looking solemn, says, "I'm afraid I have good news and bad news. Plain and simple," Steve continues, "my cousin does not want any explosives on Sicilian soil. It's very dangerous, not only to the people of Sicily, but to his reputation if something goes wrong."

"And the good news?" Jim asked Steve.

"The good news is he will arrange for the product to be gotten from the Libyans and he is content with the five-hundred thousand."

Jim took a deep breath and felt as if someone had kicked him in the stomach. Fred then said, "Wait a minute. This is actually good. Steve, your cousin arranges for us to buy the product for the one million and tells them we are Serbs or Croatians or whoever the terrorists of the month are. Let your cousin arrange for us to pick up the product there."

"I think that is a reasonable request, but I cannot answer for my cousin. I will have to go back to Sicily and ask or if I have to beg for his help, maybe you can sweeten the pot."

"If you have to," Fred says. "You be the judge, but try not to let him hold you up. We have gone too far to quit now."

Just then, Bill says, "I can't be going back again. My wife and kids are starting to ask questions."

Tom volunteers to go with Steve. "After all," he said, "I did all the research. I know where the product is and how much we are going to need."

"That will be all right," Steve says. "I have gotten comfortable enough at this point to bargain or pleas or remind my cousin that we are blood. I don't think even Tom's handsome Irish face can screw that up."

Fred remarks to the guys, "In the 1960's, Libya was our ally and as I may have told you before, we were required to land there on our way to Egypt. I was then with Military Air Transport and if I remember correctly, right outside of Tripoli is a seldom used airstrip in a somewhat deserted place called Chardemis and by jet should be around seventy-five minutes from Catania. It should be easy loading up with the product there and taking off undetected."

Jim again directs his conversation towards Steve and reminds him that the next step depends on him and, of course, Tom. Jim tells the new duo, "As soon as they get back, just call Phil and Phil will get back to both of you in person about the next meeting."

Dom arose out of his daydream and said, "This is getting more and more complicated!"

Jim says, "All hands on the table!" and they yell, "Bonus time!"

Jim looks at Dom as he's leaving and asks, "How are you feeling?"

"I told you," he said, "with my hands. Besides, what are you afraid of, that I'll die an hour before the rest of you."

Five says pass and Phil gets a call from Steve.

"We are at JFK," Steve says and hangs up. Phil calls Jim and Jim tells Phil to contact everyone personally and tell them there is a meeting tomorrow at Phil's house at ten a.m. The guys start arriving at Phil's at eight thirty a.m.. By nine o'clock, everyone is in their places around Phil's table and the next phase starts. Steve reports his cousin had made contact through one of his produce companies that was supplying fruits and vegetables to Libya.

"The price is one million American dollars and the Libyans didn't care who the fuck we were, they were agreeable to us picking up the product at that airstrip in Ghardmis, which by the way, is now abandoned." Steve went on, "My cousin also thinks we are crazy, but he admires that."

Jim interrupts Steve and asks, "Can your cousin be trusted?"

Steve replies, "It's a little too late to think of that now! But to answer your question, I believe he is a man of honor and by the way, he wants an additional one-hundred-and-fifty thousand for his troubles."

"Two things I must know," Fred said. "One, the type of jet your cousin has arranged for us. Two, how he wants his money."

Steve looked at Fred and said, "I have this information. We should arrive in Catania two days before we depart Catania. He now wants $650,000 for him, $250,000 for lease of the plane, which is a Lear Jet 35A that seats eight and cruises at 529 miles per hour. The money for my cousin should be transferred to one of his accounts at the Deutche Bank of Sicily."

Jim asks Steve, "What about the purchase of the product in

Libya?"

Steve was well prepared with answers. "The Libyans want one million American dollars for the product."

Fred stated, "We can handle that, but how do we know there won't be a double cross?"

"My cousin," Steve said, "told these guys that this was a initial order and if they wanted to do additional business, everything must go smoothly."

Dom asked, "How do we pick up the product in Libya?"

"That is arranged," Steve said. "According to my cousin, he also knew of the desolate, abandoned airstrip right outside of Ghardmis on the Tunisia border, which is approximately four-hundred-and-sixty miles from Sicily."

Fred interrupts and observes that the side trip to Libya will now cause some logistic problems and new routing. He tells the guys they may now have to fly over four countries or possibly down the Red Sea and back up the Arabian Sea. The latter, however, would drain the plane of fuel, but the chances of remaining stealth are better.

Jim tells the guys that the mission is getting more and more complicated. They all heard Fred talk about the route, the fuel and the problem of being undetected. Jim asked, "If there are any second thoughts, now is the time to back out! No questions asked." Everyone looked at each other, but so far no one wavered. So Jim went on to say, "It is now April 10th. Our departure date is May 15th! All of us should start talking at home about our upcoming baseball tour. Dom, you make sure your family hears you making inquiries about renting the tour bus. Next meeting, Tuesday, 8 p.m. at Phil's house. Make sure your minds are made up. If anyone wants to back out, Tuesday is the day."

As the guys filed out of Phil's house, the mood was somber. Everyone realized they had reached the point that this mission was definitely going to happen. Now they had to decide whether they were still men enough to carry this thing off. And, oh, yes, were they ready to leave their families and possible this world behind? Jim could feel the self-doubt rising up in him, let alone the rest of the guys. Would the families of the guys ever forgive him? They would surely know that he was the architect of this plan. How would his own family react? Would the Senior Eight be looked on as a bunch of old guys who lost their minds, or would they be looked on as heroes? Who cares, Jim thought, as long as they were capable of carrying out the mission and get the devil's descendent? Jim went home, crawled into bed and tried to sleep. Sleep was not his ally since he initiated this plan and the closer he got, the less sleep he got. When speaking amongst themselves, it was evident that sleep was not a friend of any of the guys.

The next meeting was scheduled to take place at Phil's on Tuesday. Every one of the guys was getting antsy. When Jim would speak with them, their conversations were getting abrupt. Jim felt that maybe it was just his imagination, but then he realized even he was questioning himself, so why not them? Tuesday, he felt, will answer many questions. So why try to guess?

26. WHAT TO DO? WHAT TO DO?

Director of the C.I.A. Beletta had stepped up his meeting with his inner circle of agents. He was told by agents Dee and Davis, that the old guys were now trying to acquire explosives. Belleta thought to himself that the government was going to have to move fast as these old guys had no way of knowing that the United States had been training special forces in Afghanistan to take out the evil Bin Laden. "The old guys can only get in the way, and bring unwanted attention to the location of Bin Laden". Beletta reasoned that they were going to have to give the old warriors a lot of rope before they pulled them back at the last possible moment. "How could he accomplish this without killing them?", he thought. "Who would ever believe as the C.I.A. got this close, that they would have to contend with eight fugitives from an assisted living home." Beletta also wondered how these guys were keeping their plans from their families? "Maybe the C.I.A", he smirked, "could learn from them?".

27. ANSWERS

It was now Tuesday and Steve reported everything was a go in Catania. "The plane will be fueled and ready to go May 15th. A flight plan will already be filed. The destination on paper at least will be Palermo. The connection had been made for the product with the Libyans. It will be picked up May 16th in Ghardemus at the abandoned airstrip. The product and the money will change hands as close to noon of the 16th as possible."

"How do we know they are not giving us duds?" Dom asked.

Jim told the guys, "If they gave us duds, then they were not ruled by greed and supposedly these people have been selling to terrorists all over the world and if they sold duds, they would be out of business."

Fred said, "We could fly over some desolate area and test part of the product." And if it didn't work, he was out two million dollars and then back to Palermo and ultimately to the diner and just existing again.

Tom shouted, "I'll come up with a better plan than that."

Nelse asked the guys if they thought they needed a workout before they departed. Bill did not like Nelson's use of the word 'departed' and the guys were united that they did not need a workout.

Jim again asked if any of the guys wanted to back out. "There will be no questions asked." Jim thought he saw a hesitation in Steve. Bill had told Jim that he thought Steve had fallen in love with his cousin Lucia who, as he found out, was more of a fourth or fifth cousin. Bill also thought the feeling was mutual, but Steve did not tip his hand. The guys put their hands on Phil's table and Dom yelled, "Bonus time!" so loud it startled the rest of the guys.

28. A ROYAL PAIN IN THE ASS

Belleta was thinking that while the world was getting ready to witness the Royal Wedding, he was being given a royal pain in the ass by this group of white-beards. "These guys should be thinking of Florida and early bird specials", Beletta thought. Instead, they were forcing their country into immediate action, and worst of all, they were unaware of all the trouble they were causing. Beletta was going to have to convince the President to give the okay to immediately hit Bin Laden. "The time had come", he thought, "the time was even convenient for the President. If the raid was successful, it would take the heat off the countries' many economic problems, and even boost the President's sagging ratings. The Republicans had nothing to combat that with. Besides, the time was coming fast that these ageless wonders were going to act.

29. PENNIES FROM HEAVEN

The Libyans were already talking about dividing the money. This was easy money and the best part was according to their Sicilian sources, there were plenty more transactions to come. So Omar their leader stressed to his men that everything must go well. Omar knew that some of his men wanted to shortchange the Serbs or Croatians or whoever the hell they were, but he had convinced them that this was just the beginning and that there was much more money to come. He told them how easy it would be—all they had to do is drive to the abandoned runway in Ghardemis and exchange the explosives for one million dollars of good old America money. Omar then left his men to drive the hundred miles or so to Ghardemis. He wanted to make sure the abandoned runway could still accommodate plane landings. After inspecting the runway, he was sure a small Lear jet could land comfortable there.

30. PLAY BALL!

The baseball season was starting April 5th and Jim sensed time running out. He and the guys had to deal with the idea of leaving their families and all things that they love. Most of the guys had grandchildren and some of them had very gifted grandchildren and it was becoming more and more obvious with each passing day that they might not live to see them grow up. They had a mission and all focus had to be on that. He and the guys could not go soft now. He wished it was May 14th. He was feeling queasy and was sure the rest of the guys were having trouble maintaining a good front. After all, if just one caved, they were all in trouble. Once they got started, they could leave all the lying and deceit behind them.

31. FEELING NOTHING MORE THAN FEELINGS

Dom paced back and forth. The pains in his chest started to subside. He wondered if the upcoming mission was hastening his race to life's finish line. Is this the way his life was to end, in the comfort of his home, or in some strange land whose name he only heard on the evening news? Either way, he knew his time was running out.

Phil was more determined than ever to go out with a bang. After all, his life has become so mundane that he even thought of going back with his ex-wife. At least his two kids would like that. Either way, he figured it was a death sentence.

Tom was trying to keep busy doing menial household chores. He tried not to think because when he did, he got a sinking feeling. He thought he might be old, but in his heart, he was still a marine and he wasn't about to back out of this mission.

Steve had mixed emotions for the first time since his wife had passed. He was in love with the beautiful Lucia and he was sure that in spite of their age difference, she was in love with him. This was causing second thoughts. After all, he had always lived his life without conscience. What did he really give a fuck about Bin Laden? If Jim was right, even the United States government wasn't ready to kill him. Steve had always believed that the government was no different from the mob. At least the mob had given him a living.

Nelse was busy putting things in order. He had decided to close the gym because it stopped being profitable. He told his wife when he came back from the baseball tour that he would only do private training sessions in people's homes. Then the thought raced through his head—he probably wasn't coming back. A chill went up and down his spine. Nelse knew in his heart he had to be part of this.

Fred thought, am I crazy? I finally have peace and tranquility, but that peace was shattered when the doctor told him he had a year at best to live. Life is funny, Fred thought. I have all the money I'd ever want, I have the wife of my dreams who loves me, but it's all temporary, borrowed or leased. If Jim's daughter hadn't found him, would he have been content to just wait to die? The last five years were painful. First, the quadruple bypass, then the prostate cancer, followed by a valve replacement. All this and being diabetic to boot. At least this bizarre plan by his friend Jim would provide him with the opportunity to go out like a man. Fred also knew so much of this mission revolved around him. He couldn't back out now!

Billy thought of how much his grandchildren needed him and his wife. Five years earlier, Bill's daughter lost her husband in a terrible accident. Bill stepped in and become a father figure for her children. He was there for soccer, little league and school plays. His grandchildren had become his life. What would they do without him? How would they handle losing two father figures in five years? The closer the mission got, the more trouble Bill had sleeping.

32. THE PARTY

The guys decided to have a party Saturday night, May 10th, at Viola's upstairs. All the guys made sure their entire families would be present. They sent plane tickets to those that lived far away. The theme of the party was baseball, since everyone thought this was a pre-tour party. Everyone, of course, except the Senior Eight, who knew it was more like a goodbye party. The guys did not want the party to end, but of course it had to. As everyone was leaving, Dom could be heard telling everyone the time the bus was picking them up and then whispered to each of them to make sure they had their passports. Dom also made sure to mention in front of everyone that the first stop on the tour would be Washington D.C. where they would take in a Washington-Florida baseball game. The plan was to take in two games, then have the bus driver taken them to Dulles Airport where they would leave for Catania. The bus driver would be paid to lay low for a few days. In fact, Jim instructed him to drive to Philadelphia as if they were still with him. The second stop was supposed to be a Phillie-Mets game. At this time, the bus driver was instructed to return the bus and report the rest of the tour was cancelled. By this time, Jim figured they would be ready to leave Catania and no one could possibly stop them. The wives of the guys were kidding each other. One of them observed, "I've heard of a midlife crisis, but I think they are having an end-of-life crisis!" Little did the women know how accurate that statement was! After all, that was the motivational factor that started this whole adventure.

33. AND NOW IT BEGINS

May 12th came. The guys all met at Phil's place and boarded the bus for Washington. Jim surveyed the guys as they stepped onto the bus. Dom's color, he thought, was somewhat ashen. Nelson still looked fit and at least ten years younger than his age. Steve looked deep in thought and Billy was exceedingly nervous. Tommy had that crazed look which all the guys were familiar with. Phil excused himself to go to the bathroom. Fred was busy studying his notes and navigational routes and Jim himself couldn't stop his knees from shaking. This was it! Everyone was sitting comfortably on the bus. Next stop, Washington's Holiday Inn, where they would spend the night. They would then see two baseball games and on May 12th, would board an Al Italia plane for Catania. They would spend a night in Catania at two different hotels, both far away from Steve's family, as requested by Steve's cousin Marco. Marco's second request was that once there, only Steve should contact him and that was only to make sure that all the money was there. Marco in no uncertain terms made sure Steve understood that he wanted no contact with the rest of the group.

The Senior Eight arrived at the Holiday Inn, settled in and then left for the beautiful new Washington Stadium. They took their seats and tried to enjoy the ballgame, but enjoyment was not coming easy for any of them. That night, they decided to skip the second game and go from the Holiday Inn directly to Dulles Airport. They boarded Al Italia flight 121 and the guys were on their way to Catania.

34. MONEY! MONEY! MAKES THE WORLD GO ROUND!

Jim asked Fred if he was sure the money was transferred to the Deutche Bank of Catania to Marco's account. Fred assured Jim this had been done and that they had come too far to screw up now. The guys, who were always very vocal, seemed to turn into mimes. Only their breathing assured Jim that they were still alive. Eyes were glassy and the mood was tense. Jim again began to think ...how would these old-school grandfathers hold up under this extraordinary pressure? Would they have what it takes to complete this mission, or would they fall apart? After all, they averaged seventy years of age and two operations, each over the last six years. Jim reasoned they would soon find out. The plane was now past the halfway point and Jim's heart started beating faster. He began to doubt himself. He thought, did he—the architect, the big mouth, the super salesman, the driving force of this operation—have the balls? He thought the way he felt now was scared, almost numb! He knew he had to come out of this. The guys needed him. He had to put on a brave front, not show how scared he was!

It was getting closer and closer to put up time. Very little communicating among the guys was done on the plane. They were now three quarters of the way to Sicily. Dom still didn't look good and Fred was studying his notes. After all, ultimately the success of the mission depended on him! Billy looked like he wanted to say something, but didn't. Steve just looked straight ahead. Phil was the only one that seemed to have a slight smile on his face. Tom had that same determined look on his face that he had when they were young and he was about to get into a fight. Nelse was expressionless, looking straight ahead, almost as if he were praying. Jim thought, when this whole thing started four months ago, would anyone have thought that they would even get this far? He then decided to break the tension, check with each guy to see if they were taking their medication. Phil had the best remark. "Why are you checking on us? Are you afraid we are going to die?"

35. IT'S 9 A.M., DO YOU KNOW WHERE YOUR HUSBAND IS?

There was a strong knock on the door of Myrtle Kellerher's colonial ranch, followed by the ring of the bell. Myrtle had been getting dressed and had a luncheon appointment with the wives of all the guys on the tour. She was a little hesitant in answering the bell. It was still very early in the morning and she was alone, but then curiosity overcame fear and she answered the door. On the outside were two average looking fortyish men in dark suits.

"Mrs. Kellerher," they said. Myrtle's first thought was, oh my God! Something happened to her husband! The two suits immediately assured her that nothing has happened. They were just following up on something that perhaps she could shed some light on.

"Are you the police?" Myrtle asked

"No, not exactly, but let us show you our identification."

Myrtle became even more startled when she saw Federal Bureau of Investigation. Her tone became more demanding. "What is this about?"

"Mrs. Kellerher, we would like to have a few words with your husband," came the reply.

"My husband is with his friends touring baseball parks!" Myrtle answered. "So you will have to wait a month!"

"Mrs. Kellerher, do you know why your husband has been buying books about explosives?"

"I have no idea what you are talking about and you are getting me very upset!" Myrtle replied.

The two agents realized that the questioning was about to get them thrown out of the house, so they announced that they would be leaving, but would appreciate her making a list of the people her husband was with and to include their telephone numbers and addresses. They thanked her in advance and then left.

36. SUNNY SICILY

The plane was now nearing Fontarossa Airport in Catania. The guys would land there and four of them would head for the Central Palace Hotel and four would go to the Hotel Gresi. Jim thought by splitting the guys up, they would be less noticeable. So Steve, Billy, Nelse and Tom would head to Central Palace and Jim, Dom, Phil and Fred to the Hotel Gresi.

All of a sudden, there was a loud thunderclap and lightning was everywhere. At times, the plane was lit up like a Christmas tree. Dom whispered to Jim, "What a cruel trick of fate this would be if the plane crashes."

Jim was having the exact same thought and as he looked at the rest of the guys was pretty sure they were also thinking the same thing. Suddenly, the pilot's voice came on the loudspeaker. According to the captain, the computers indicated that the landing gear was not coming down! They were going to pass by the observation tower so they could eyeball the plane and see if the landing gear was down. The observation tower confirmed the landing gear was down, so the pilot got back on the loudspeaker and announced the good news, saying it was probably just a computer error.

"However," he said, "There is a slight chance the landing gear might not be locked."

The plane landed on the emergency runway surrounded by the flashing lights of many emergency vehicles. There were many sighs of, "Thank God!" and the passengers broke out in applause. Everyone seemed to be thanking God except Fred. Fred wanted to know why God—if there was a God, which he doubted—has to put us through this. At least Fred was consistent with his atheist beliefs. Fred compounded his remark with, "We don't have time for this God stuff! We have a job to do and we can't stop to figure out whose side God is on or if their God is better than your God."

Jim said, "Enough, Fred. You made your point." Jim had a flashback of when he and Fred were kids and Fred would try to bait Jim's aunts who were religious into a debate on religion, telling them his uncle had a heart attack because God made his grass grow and while cutting it, he died. Jim's aunts would just make the sign of the cross and look the other way. Later, they would ask Jim why he hung around with such a person. The next time Jim and Fred were alone, he asked Fred to refrain from engaging his aunts in any type of religious discussions, but of course he didn't. The ironic thing was that in later life, it was Fred the atheist that did more for the underprivileged regardless of race or religion, than all of so-called religious friends and relatives, highlighted by his march arm and arm on Washington with Martin Luther King Jr. Fred indeed was a complex individual!

37. CONFUSION EVERYWHERE

The two F.B.I. agents returned to their office to fill out a report on their visit to the Kellerher residence. Neither one of them thought that there was any reason for concern, but the clerk at Borders Bookstore had called their office and reported Tom Kellerher as suspicious and edgy. Little did they know that this young clerk had Tom summed up perfectly, but the agents both figured he did not fit the profile of a terrorist. However, they would keep the case open and perhaps follow up on that baseball tour when they picked up the list of Tom's companions.

That afternoon, Myrtle met the wives for lunch. The topic they were supposed to discuss was a cruise together when their husbands got back. They were happy that their husbands were doing something they loved. They figured when they came home that they could all plan a cruise together. After all, how could they say no? As the girls met, before any discussion of a cruise could get started, Myrtle told the women of the strange visit she'd had that morning and about the two men identifying themselves as Federal agents and asking questions about Tom's interest in explosives and where he was and they asked for a list of the men he was on the tour with.

Jim's wife Lynn asked, "What else did they say?"

Myrtle answered that she was very nervous, but she remembered they said they would be back within the week. "I did ask them why they were so interested in my husband and his friends and their baseball tour. They said it was just routine."

Suddenly, the women were almost catatonic, looking at each other in disbelief.

"This can't be happening," Dom's wife, Marie, said, over and over.

Coleen, Nelson's wife, remembered mood swings over the last month, but she thought it was because he had to close the gym. Billy's wife Joyce observed strange behavior of her husband lately. Fred's wife Grace said Fred was always studying books and notes lately, but she thought he was studying the stock market. Jim's wife Lynn thought her husband's mood swings were because of the dismal start the Mets got off to. Then all the women, almost simultaneously, realized something was wrong. They began to compare notes and they shockingly realized that almost to a man, their husbands recently revised their wills. They decided to call the Holiday Inn in Washington and try to get to the bottom of this. Numerous calls were made, but none were answered.

The girls decided to meet every day and be a support system for each other. They now realized something was terribly wrong, but what? Explosives? What would they be doing with explosives? The girls knew their husbands were for the most part patriotic to a fault and they were definitely law-abiding. The girls were dazed and confused. They couldn't tell anybody for fear that would be jeopardizing their husbands and whatever the hell they may be doing. They were all convinced that their husbands must believe in what they were doing, but why now, at this age, would they jeopardize everything? It was like a bad dream. It just didn't make sense, but they all realized there was a plan. No one answered phone calls and none of the men had checked in with their wives. They all felt as if they were in *The Twilight Zone*.

38. YOU GO YOUR WAY, WE'LL GO OURS

As the guys broke into two groups with Jim, Fred, Dom and Phil catching a taxi to the Hotel Gresi, while Steve, Bill, Nelse and Tom headed for the Central Palace Hotel. After Jim and the guys got settled at the Gresi, they had the opportunity to go voer some last minute details. Jim asked Fred questions on flying time, weather conditions, altitudes, flying below the radar and most importantly at this time, Fred being able to transfer the money that they needed. Fred reiterated to Jim that he went to the Deutch Bank of New York and transferred the money to the Deutch Bank of Catania. Jim then asked Fred if he was questioned as to why he was moving such a large amount of money out of the country. Fred had the answer, telling the bank exec that he was thinking of retiring there and would like to buy some property. This dove tailed well with Steve's cousin Marco, who owned many businesses, not only in Sicily, but also in mainland Italy and more than a few were real estate businesses.

Back at the Central Palace, Steve's cell phone rang and it was Jim.

"Tell the guys to be at Flynn's Irish Pub in Catania at eight p.m. tonight."

Flynn's was a celebrated Irish pub in Catania. It was one of the three Irish pubs that flourished in Catania. That night as the guys settled in at Flynn's, Jim offered a toast to all their families and to the country they loved, America. A second round of drinks was ordered and some beef and lamb dishes for the guys to dine on. The only one that wasn't happy was Tom, who was Irish, but kept muttering, "We are in Italy. Why are we not eating Italian?"

Jim replied, "We always eat Italian at home. I figured this would be different and I didn't think you of all people would object." Jim then asked Steve to make sure his cousin Marco knew that they were all there and so was the money. Steve had to make sure his cousin Marco could be trusted because if Marco fucked them, it was all over. The mission was dead and Fred was out two million dollars—a certified check for $1,900,000. $650,000 for Marco and $250,000 for lease of the plane and one million in cash to be turned over to Steve for purchase of the product. The other $100,000 was brought to Catania in American Express checks, which would be used for miscellaneous expenses: hotels, tips and any unforeseen expenses.

A third round of drinks were ordered and the guys became a little more relaxed. It was then that Steve blurted out the he wasn't going. Steve said he decided to stay back and make sure his cousin Marco does everything he's supposed to do. Jim looks at Steve and asks, "Is that the only reason you're staying back?"

Steve was honest and told the guys that he fell in love with his cousin Lucia and now he felt like living again. "Forgive me, guys, but that is the way it is."

The guys looked at each other, somewhat shocked, but Jim had sensed Steve was weakening. Love is a very strong adversary, Jim thought.

Just then, the second blow was delivered. Billy said he wasn't going, either. He went on to say his second thoughts started on the plane. He thought of his grandchildren who six short years ago lost their father and Bill had stepped in and attended their little league games, soccer and school plays. Billy had become their father and how would they deal with losing two fathers in the span of six years? He just couldn't do that to them.

Not one of the guys could fault Billy for feeling that way, and so now they were down to six.

39. DETAILS! DETAILS!

The following morning, Steve made the journey to Taormina to see cousin Marco. They had completed the bank transactions and Marco received his $750,000. The money was deposited in the Deutschland bank account for Taormina Produce, one of Marco's exporting companies. Steve returned and assured the guys that Marco was to be trusted. Jim then asked Bill and Steve to stay in Catania until after the mission was completed. Both agreed and Steve remarked that he was going to spend the rest of his days in Sicily. Steve then relayed the details of his conversation with cousin Marco. The plane was fueled up and awaited them in Hanger #7 at the Fontanarossa airport. A flight plan had been filed from Catania to Palermo. Everything now was in Fred's hands—the takeoff navigation, the landing in Libya and ultimately the target in Pakistan. Fred was still studying maps and navigational routes, altitudes and various ways to go undetected by radar. Jim thought of the incredible pressure on Fred, a man who was given just one year to live.

It was now only twenty-four hours from takeoff time. Jim and Fred went to the airport to check out the Lear jet. Fred did not want any surprises. He seemed very happy with what he had been inspecting. He remarked to Jim that the plane was exactly like the schematic he had been studying. Jim breathed a sigh of relief and they both headed back to the hotel.

They scheduled the final meeting before takeoff at the pub and then the following morning 10 a.m. takeoff time, destination Ghardamis, Libya. It was almost a moral victory getting even this far, but the guys were not interested in moral victories. They wanted Satan's kid, Bin Laden. The guys were very pensive, almost numb.

Bill and Steve were torn. They had gone this far, but both had excellent reasons to go no further. Dom was seen grabbing his chest and Nelse always seemed to be praying. Tom looked half-crazed like a man about to come out of his skin. Phil looked relaxed and ready to go. Fred was intent reading maps, getting weather reports and studying the schematic of the Lear jet they were going to board.

40. It's Too Late Now!

Jim thought, what has he gotten these guys into? At a time when they should be playing checkers at some senior citizens center and wondering what they were going to eat for dinner and what they were going to argue about with their wives, instead Jim had them plotting how they were going to turn themselves into weapons and how they most probably would be spending the last two days of their lives. Jim also wondered if Fred was right and there was no God. On that score, Jim hoped Fred was wrong, but they were probably about to find out.

That night when they went to bed, none of them could sleep. The sun took forever to rise that morning. Finally daylight filled Jim's room and all eight of the guys met at the airport. As they all gathered at the airport, the tension could be cut with a knife. Bill was still feeling guilty about not going, but Steve was very comfortable with his decision and had no regrets. All eight guys hugged and Dom yelled, "Let's do it!"

Tears welled up in Bill's eyes.

41. It Takes Two To Tango

Omar Hassad and Quadhafi were children together growing up in Libya that was then ruled b y the British. They played together, begged for food together and in their teenage years even made love to the same women. It was then that Quadhafi started a revolutionary cell and naturally Omar was at his side. When they were both 27 years old, they successfully overthrew the puppet regime and took over the country. Quadhafi wasn't through. He stared sponsoring international terrorism and Omar became his instrument of mayhem. Omar was the man behind the Lockerbie bombing and everyone in the middle-east knew it. When the United States placed sanctions on Libya, it was Omar who secured all kinds of product, not only from the rogue Russians, but also through a very powerful man in Sicily who provided a steady flow of food stuffs, mainly produce, into Libya.

42. Handle With Care

Omar and his band of terrorists were getting ready for an easy payday, carefully picking up explosives form Omar's warehouse just outside of Tripoli. Omar cautioned his men to handle the explosives carefully. He watched as the sweat poured from the bodies of his six men. The temperature had reached 118 degrees that day and even with a slight breeze coming off the Mediterranean, it was still unbearably hot. Libya, had after all, recorded the hottest temperature ever; 136 degrees Fahrenheit Heat and lack of water have always been Libya's nemesis.

Although Libya had become an oil rich nation in the late 1950s, it still had to import much of its fruits and vegetables and there lied the connection with Steve's cousin Marco. Marco was very happy to fill that void for the Libyans. The sanctions placed on Libya proved to be very profitable for Marco and for his many businesses. Money makes strange bedfellows. In the not so distant past, Italy had ruled Libya and subjected Libyans to slave-like conditions, and now Libya was importing fruits and vegetables and through those connections, Omar was securing a huge payday for him and his men, even after kicking back $500,000 to his mentor Quadhafi and his military. Omar knew all terrorists based in Libya had to kickback to Quadhafi's military! The military had so much money to buy arms that they had five times the guns and ammo than its soldiers could use in two lifetimes. Quadhafi knew Omar well. They had a mutual respect for each other. Omar also knew that he had to stay in line and kickback part of everything he earned through his terrorists activities. Omar financed Quadhafi's personal terrorist attacks such as the Pan American Flight 103 that on December 21, 1988, he blew up, killing 259 people.

Now 22 years later, Omar and his band of terrorists were hours away from meeting head on with the white-haired grand-fatherly six, who were about to turn over one million dollars to them. Omar was still unclear as to who these people were, but as long as the money was good, that's all he really cared about. He didn't give a shit whether they were Croatians, Serbs or even extra terrestrials, as long as he got the money.

The following morning could not come fast enough for Omar. He was astute enough to realize that this deal had to go down as advertised. Quadhafi was very aware as to what Omar was doing—he had to make Quadhafi aware of everything he and his men did. Those that didn't had a habit of disappearing and there was no other political group that opposed Quadhafi. Omar knew as long as the Libyan economy was so dependent on its oil that if the price of oil dropped dramatically, then and only then would Quadhafi have major problems. Omar also was very politically aware and knew that Quadhafi was schizo-phrenic. After all, hadn't he declared war on surrounding coun-tries such as Chad for no given reason? Omar quickly dismissed these thoughts. He had to focus on the job at hand.

43. UP! UP! AND AWAY!

Fred briefed Jim on the flight plan that had already been filed, evidently by Steve's cousin Marco. Their supposed destination was Palermo, but Fred explained, "We will fly past there to Libya. The entire flight should take less than one hour. We then fly over the sea at about five-hundred feet altitude to Ghardemis, Libya." At that point, Fred explained, "The authorities at the Palermo Airport would try to track them to find out whether we crashed or landed somewhere. Hopefully they will lose sight of us on their radar while we continue to Libya, which should be another one hour flight past Palermo. Once we land in Ghardemis, the fun really starts. It is kaopectate time."

Jim then asked Fred if they flew at five-hundred feet, what are the chances thjey could avoid radar?

"Well!" Fred said. "It definitely will minimize the chances of them picking us up and better you ask me if I have ever flown at five-hundred feet. The answer is yes. Five-hundred feet," Fred continued, "is roughly the height of the Verrazano Bridge."

Jim looked at Fred and couldn't help but think that Fred looked like he'd aged five years in the last two days. The burden of this whole mission sat squarely on his shoulders and Fred was beginning to look worn down.

It was now time for all the guys to board the plane. Jim checked everything and everyone around him. He remembered the words of one of the old mustached Pete's where he grew up in East New York. The old guy would say, "Kid, don't trust anyone. That way, you'll never be disappointed."

44. SURPRISE! SURPRISE!

The two F.B.I. agents returned to Tom and Myrtle Kellerher's house and picked up the list of addresses and phone numbers of all the guys Tom was with on the baseball tour. When they called Dom Faella's house, they found out from his wife Marie the name of the bus company (Fuccillo Buses) that they hired for their tour. They were fast to interview Raymond Fuccillo the president and then were taken aback to find out the bus and the driver had returned! Fuccillo spilled everything to the Feds about the bus and the driver being paid in advance for one month, then after two days, the driver was tipped handsomely to keep his mouth shut and was told they did not need his bus or services any longer. He then dropped them at Dulles Airport at Al Italia departures and came back to the bus lot the next day. The Feds immediately made Fuccillo contact the driver and bring him into the office. Under cross-examination, it was evident the driver knew nothing, but one thing he did observe was that for a bunch of guys on holiday, they certainly seemed kind of tense and quiet. The Feds were sure at this point that these old guys were up to something big, but what? It still made no sense to them!

45. IN UNITY, THERE'S STRENGTH

Myrtle called all the women to her house and brought them up to date on the new developments. It was now four days since any of them had spoken to their husbands. They were all visibly shaken, but still agreed not to say anything to anyone. If they needed to talk, it would only be to each other. The women threw around a lot of guesses as to what their men were up to, but one thing was for sure—they knew whatever it was, it was big and bad and they might never see them again. The women decided to go home, get clothes and return to Myrtle's house until they got some news. They all told their children where they could be reached and that Myrtle wasn't feeling well! They were going to spend a few days with her.

46. TO MOVE OR NOT TO MOVE

Back at the military base in Pakistan, the Pakistani generals had just completed a meeting on what to do with their cash cow, Bin Laden. Those drone missiles that the United States was launching were coming awfully close to their base. The generals thought that maybe there was a change of mind in the American government and maybe, they felt, it was time to do away with Bin Laden. The generals knew the last suicide bombing that took the lives of six C.I.A. agents could have been the strand that broke the camel's back. The generals were divided as to whether they should find a new place to stash Bin Laden. Bin Laden himself had become a twenty-four hour project, needing constant medical care and even with that, he seemed to be deteriorating rapidly. The I.S.I. and the Pakistani generals knew they must keep him alive. He generated more money for them that than they ever could have imagined. They knew if he died, their good times were over! No more Saudi money and definitely no more billions from the Unites States.

47. WHERE'S THE JUSTICE?

The Senior Six were now all aboard the Lear jet. Fred was in the cockpit continuing to familiarize himself with the controls. Jim's thoughts went to Steve's cousin Marco. What if the plane blew up? All evidence would be destroyed! Cousin Marco would be off the hook, $650,000 richer, plus maybe even the insurance on the plane. Then he realized they had one million dollars on the plane and if Marco intended to blow up the plane, he would have found a way to keep the million dollars. Jim then ran to the attaché case, opened it up and was relieved the money was still there. Jim decided it was too late to worry about Marco, and all his energy should be directed toward the mission. Then he started thinking about his family that he loved, but would probably never see again. He had to dismiss these thoughts and get back to what was now real! Were he and his guys capable of finishing this mission?

Just then, Fred heard in his earphones for flight Cinque Una to taxi to runway Dui Uno for clearance to take off for Palermo. All the guys stiffened up as they knew this was it. Jim thought he was born on the day Pearl Harbor was bombed by an enemy and now he would probably die bombing an enemy. How appropriate is that? Who says there is no justice?

48. WHO? WHAT? WHY?

The agents hastily called a meeting with their superiors. They knew something was going on, but they couldn't imagine what. They briefed their superiors, they briefed Homeland Security, but the only real information that they had received was from Al Italia Airlines that the eight old guys left on their Flight 116 for Catania, Sicily. No one in any of the security agencies had any idea of what these guys has in mind. They kept going over the facts: one, eight guys lied to their wives about a baseball tour they had no intention of completing. Two, they were now in Catania, Sicily. Three, they obviously had some type of plan. Four, Italian immigration officials had logged them through Catania hours earlier. No eyebrows were raised, and airport authorities were sure they weren't armed in any way. So what the hell were these guys up to and who, if anybody, were they working for? Something was fishy. The books on explosives. The phony baseball tour. The payoff to the bus driver. The consensus of the people attending the meeting was to call Italian authorities and locate and detain these old timers for questioning. The American agencies were shocked to find out that these guys were no longer in Catania and a plane had been leased at the Fontarosa Airport for them and as far as the Italian authorities knew, they were on their way to Palermo and one of the old guys was piloting the plane. The plot was thickening and histories of all the guys were searched for and found and there it was: Lt. Fredrick Santos, Pilot, Strategic Air Command. Who the hell are these guys? And what are they up to? Italian authorities were told when the plane lands in Palermo, detain the plane and everyone on it.

49. GOODBYE, PALERMO

Fred was talking to the Palermo Borsellino Airport, receiving landing instructions. Fred turned to Jim and said, "Here we go!" Fred dropped down to five-hundred feet, went right by Palermo and over the Mediterranean. The guys were all huddled together watching the Palermo skyline go by.

Jim looked at Fred and said, "There ain't no stopping us now."

Fred did not answer, but started to burp profusely. Finally, he said, "We didn't accomplish anything yet. The best is yet to come!" The he seemed to be taking deep breaths. Jim thought the pressure on Fred must be unbelievable. He was the pilot, the navigator, all this pressure on a guy that had quadruple bypass, a new heart valve, prostate cancer, diabetes and a forecast of one year to live from his doctor. What had he done to these guys, to their families, all on a fifty-fifty chance at best that they could destroy the monster of the Mid East? Fred then groaned and Jim asked, "Are you okay?"

Fred replied, "Just a little indigestion from all the wrong food I've been eating. Why we couldn't have had Italian food while we were in Italy, I'll never know!"

The groans coming from Fred were more frequent. Jim again asked Fred if he was okay. Fred abruptly told Jim, "Go to the back of the plane and talk to the guys." He didn't need a mother standing next to him.

Jim walked to the cabin and spoke with the guys, to a man he could feel the tension! Tom had whipped himself into a frenzy and Phil made a curious remark. He said, "I'm glad this is almost over."

Dom tried to inject some humor. He wondered out loud if anything happened to him and his kids had more children, would they still name them Domenick or Dominique? All the guys looked at Dom and smiled. Dom wanted to know what everybody was smiling about, he was being serious!

Jim remarked, "Don't worry, Dom! Marie will keep them in line. She might even change her name to Dominique."

This time, all the guys broke into laughter. Fred then called Jim to the cockpit. He told Jim they were ten minutes from Ghardamis and Fred asked Jim to relay that information to the rest of the guys. Fred also told Jim to tell the guys that when the plane lands, to stay put. The plan was for Fred and Jim to get out of the plane and complete the transaction for the product.

50. LEAN ON ME

The women sat around the table at Myrtle's house, chatting nervously. There was a feeling that time was running out. The agents visited them and warned them that if they were withholding any information, they would all be charged with aiding and abetting. The agents also made them aware that their husbands hijacked a plane in Catania, flew over Palermo and disappeared off radar. The women seemed to all shriek at once, "Hijack a plane? That's crazy!"

The agents looked at the women and said, "What? What they have done so far is sane?" The agents themselves didn't believe the hijacking bullshit, but this is what was being told to them by the Sicilian authorities, but anyone with half a brain knew that if a flight plan had been filed, how could it be termed a hijacking?

The agents left the house pretty sure that the women were as baffled as they were. The women were now more frightened than ever and at this point, decided to go to their homes, call their children and let them know what was happening. They felt the more people to lean on, the better.

51. NOW A WORD FROM THE PRESIDENT

Italian authorities notified Washington that the flight they were tracking was given landing instructions. They dropped down as if they were landing and then disappeared off the radar screen. Everyone from the F.B.I. to the C.I.A. to the President of the United States were now aware that there were some senior Americans somewhere off the coast of Palermo that were hell bent on doing something, but what? As far as anyone knew, they were not armed and had no weapons of destruction, so what could they possibly be up to? The president was furious. He wanted to know how this could happen and ultimately, he wanted these guys stopped. He also made the clichéd remark that, "Heads would roll when this was all over. All agencies were now on high alert. This whole thing has already proved very embarrassing. If these geezers accomplish whatever they are up to, only God knows the consequences!"

A big decision had to be made. Do they alert the governments in that area of the world, or does the United States itself scramble some fighter planes from off the many aircraft carriers in the area and if they do that, what instructions would be given? Some people in Washington wanted the plane shot down—that, of course, was if they could find it.

52. WHAT THE FUCK?

Mike Dee and Scott Davis informed their boss Beletta that the old guys were now in the air and on their way. Not even the C.I.A. knew that their first step was war torn Libya, where the old boys were picking up explosives while Beletta was being informed that a satellite had tracked the seniors plane to Libya. An out of breath, overweight agent burst into the directors office and informed him about the Libya stop. Beletta looked at his people and yelled, "What the Fuck!", which was totally out of character for the man. He immediately got on the phone with the President, and asked for permission for the special forces to attack the Bin Laden compound. It seemed Bin Laden was moved out of his base at his own insistence, and moved to a specially built walled residence only 200 yards away. The President said, "Do it". The next step would be reeling in the old bastards.

53. IF IT TAKES FOREVER, I'M NOT WAITING!

Omar and his band of six had been waiting at least two hours before they spotted the Lear jet that was still far enough away and low enough that it looked like a large seagull skimming the shimmering sea. They pulled the truck up to the end of the abandoned landing strip.

Fred spotted the land and told Jim, "Remember, when we land, we spend as little time making the transaction. No questions, no answers, no nothing. They hand over the explosives, we hand over the money, and we are out of there."

The landing gear comes down as the plane descends to the abandoned landing strip. The Libyan leader Omar could already see his riches in front of him. He and his six men watched as the plane descended, then landed and taxied to the end of the abandoned runway. Omar's men instinctively gripped their machine guns more tightly as the door to the plane opened. Jim and Fred exited the plane. Not sixty feet from the truck, Omar had positioned his men, two to the left side of the truck, two to the right side and two in the back of the truck. Omar would greet his fellow terrorists or whoever the hell they were and make sure the money was there. As Jim and Fred walked up to Omar, their clothes were immediately soaked in sweat. They felt like they had stepped into a sauna.

Omar said something to the two men, who just nodded. Jim showed Omar the attaché case, opened it and the money was plainly visible. Omar's eyes looked like two street lamps. It was obvious he was pleased. Omar then nodded to the two men in the back of the truck. They took two large cases to the side of the plane, handling them very gingerly. They were so cautious that Jim worried about how easily this stuff could explode. Jim and Fred immediately handed the product to Dom and Nelson at the side exit door, telling them to be extremely careful. Jim turned around and saw Omar hunched over the attaché case, counting the money. He then stood up erect, nodded to his men, then looked at Jim and Fred and with a wave of his hand, signaled them that they could leave. Not two minutes later, all the guys were on the plane and the side exit door of the plane was shut.

Fred looked at Jim and said, "That was a lot easier than I expected. We didn't have to say a word."

Jim replied, "I guess it's true!"

"What's that?" Fred asked.

"Money talks!" Jim said, and evidently very loud. As Fred got ready to take off, Jim walked to the back of the plane where the guys were looking at the product. Tom had done his homework and done it well. The product was just as he said, wrapped in plastic just like giant Hershey bars. Fred started his take off when Tom's violent nature surfaced. He was agitated and told Jim they had to circle back. He was screaming, "We don't know what we just bought! For all we know, we have a couple of cases of candy!"

Jim protested, "Tom, the product is just as you described it."

"That don't mean shit," Tom yelled. "Tell Fred to circle back." Fred could hear Tom plainly from where he was in the cockpit. Tom again yelled at Jim, "Tell Fred to turn around!"

Jim went up front to tell Fred to turn around. Fred looked at Jim as if Jim was as crazy as Tom. "Why does he want us to turn around?" Fred asked.

Tom then came into the cockpit and screamed, "Turn this fucking plane around!"

"Why?" asked Fred.

"Because," Tom said, "we are going to test the product and see if it's real."

Fred yelled, "On what?"

Tom said, "On the Libyans."

The guys all looked at each other. Tom was sometimes crazy,

but never stupid. Jim told Fred, "Do as he says."

Fred leveled off the plane and then turned back. As Fred started to descend, the Libyans became visible. They seemed to be in the same spot, celebrating, smoking cigars and drinking, leaning against the truck. Then Omar noticed the plane coming back. He immediately sensed something was wrong. He positioned his men to fire at the plane. Omar's sixth sense had told him these guys were too old to be terrorists, but the money made him euphoric, blinding him to the danger signs.

The plane was now getting very low in the sky. Tom apparently had known what he wanted to do long before they set down in Libya. He had diesel oil and rags and he instructed the guys to wrap one pound of the explosives in a rag. According to what Tom had read, this type of explosive should detonate on impact, but Tom wasn't taking any chances. He took the diesel oil and poured some over the explosives wrapped in rags. The plane was now low and close enough to the Libyans, not two-hundred feet above them. Omar was taking no chances. He ordered his men to fire on the plane. There was pinging noises all over the plane. Tommy took out his lighter, ignited the rags that served as fuses and with Fred's guidance, dropped the explosives. It wasn't an exact hit, but it was close enough. The entire area exploded.

Tom was jumping up and down yelling, "You don't fuck with a Marine, you sons of bitches! This is payback for all the pain you caused the families of that Pan American flight."

Tom was in a frenzy. The rest of the guys just looked at him in stunned silence. Everyone on the plane watched the destruction that just a pound of these explosives caused. They all were so intent on watching that Fred almost lost control of the plane.

Tom was still yelling, "These fucking lowlifes will not be supplying terrorists anymore."

Nelson broke the silence of him and the rest of the guys saying, "I guess they didn't sell us duds."

Dom said, "They probably wished they had!"

Jim told the guys, "Don't feel bad. We just expelled them to their seventy virgins each."

Fred pulled the head of the plane up and now it was time for, as Steve would have said, the Big Hit.

54. DECISIONS! DECISIONS!

Satellite monitoring allowed American Intelligence to start piecing together what happened in Libya. The Libyan government knew almost immediately something had gone wrong. Omar had been able to send a text message to Tripoli saying he believed he and his men were about to be attacked by the people he just sold explosives to. The American government was now sure the seniors were bent on destruction , but of what? The Libyan government went into a defensive mode claiming that a small jet probably from the west had killed seven innocent people. The Libyan Ambassador went as far as saying the plane might have been manned by American mercenaries. It was becoming clear someone in Marco's organization had to have leaked information to the Libyans. American Intelligence was still trying to figure out what these old guys had done and what their next step would be. One thing though was certain, there was growing respect among some of the intelligence community. America had three aircraft carriers in the area and some members of the intelligence suggest that they scramble some fighter planes and intercept the old warriors and if necessary, shoot them down. That would end the never ending guessing and intrigue. But a minority of the group wanted to see how far the old guys could go. There was still another plan considered and that was to alert the countries in that area such as Iran, Pakistan and Afghanistan and give them permission to take any step they deemed necessary. This would prove that regardless of the goals these guys might have, the American government was innocent of any knowledge of what these old fanatical "extremists" might do. It was apparent to some in the Intelligence committee that these old guys were on a suicide mission, but what was there final destination and where? The old guys had to also make some decisions. Fred was positive now that fuel was going to be an issue. They now had to fly over three countries to get to their target. It was a shorter distance going over Syria, Iraq and Iran, but thanks to their side trip and dropping explosives on Omar in Libya, these countries Fred figured these countries had to be on alert.

Fred checked his maps and thought their best chance was to fly over water for as long as possible. He figured their best bet was to fly down the Red Sea to the Arabian Sea and back up along the Pakistani-Afghan border. This, Fred told Jim, was the best chance they had of completing the mission. The downside was their fuel would be compromised. They looked at each other and without saying a word, they knew there would be no trip back and over the water they headed.

Jim went back to the cabin to tell the guys of the decision. They were already numb and no one protested, even after Jim told them about the fuel crisis. Then Nelse brought up an interesting point. He took Jim to the storage area of the plane and showed him four parachutes that Jim and Fred had seen, but hadn't given it any thought. Nelse pointed out if things started to go awry, some of the guys could elect to take their chances on the ground. Jim immediately thought this was an option none of them had considered, and that jumping out of the plane would take a completely new set of balls.

Jim went back to the cockpit and told Fred of Nelse's discovery of the parachutes. Fred told Jim he thought of that, but he would have to give the guys a class on parachuting and he didn't have time for that! Fred then grabbed his chest and started burping again and his color seemed to be pale gray. Jim feared the worst. Just then, Fred seemed to rebound as he pointed out to Jim that they were now over the Red Sea. Jim looked down and felt he could almost touch the waves. Fred also pointed out in the distance, barely visible, was the Egyptian coast on one side and the Saudi Arabian on the other.

55. SO WHAT'S UP?

As Bill and Steve left their room at the Central Palace Hotel, they were greeted by the Carbanieri and ushered into a banquet room where intense questioning followed. Bill pretended he didn't speak Italian and Steve did not have to pretend as much. Bill's dumb act allowed him to stall for the time and meanwhile listen to the Italian being spoken. It was clear to him that the mission and the guys had been exposed. The Italian police then rushed in an English-speaking interrogator who informed them they were being held at the request of the United States government and he made sure to drive home that the United States was not happy with what was unfolding. He asked Bill and Steve to make things easier and tell him where his friends were headed and why. Billy and Steve continued to play dumb with Billy even saying that the reason they were still in Catania was because they were kept in the dark regarding the final details and decided not to go. The Italian interrogator was not buying any of it. Steve was nervous and thinking, what happens if they draw his cousin Marco into this?

The questioning continued for hours, but the old guys were maintaining their silence. Then the Italian police parted as three men approached. They identified themselves as being with the American Embassy and they were all going to be there until they decided to come clean.

Billy looked at Steve and blurted out, "We'd better go back upstairs and get our pajamas."

The suits from the embassy did not like that remark at all. One of them barked, "You guys think you're patriotic? Well, you're only screwing up and that area is screwed up enough! So save us all some time and tell us what's up!"

56. DISSENSION IN THE RANKS

The majority of people within the C.I.A. and the President's advisors wanted our allies such as Pakistan to be brought up to date on everything, including the possible tracking of the Lear jet and its has-been crew. After all, the United States had an important relationship with the Pakistani republic since its beginning almost sixty years ago. America did not want to jeopardize the relationship with Pakistan.

The President's advisors were firm in their stance that they wanted this perceived good relationship to continue into the future. They thought that Pakistan was taking firm actions on the War on Terror and it was within the United States's interest to share all information in that area of the world. They considered the Pakistanis a major non-NATO ally. This allowed Pakistan to be the recipient of arms such as tanks and fighter planes. However, within the C.I.A., there was the minority that felt Pakistan was playing both sides in the War on Terror.

57. IF THEY COULD SEE US NOW

Jim thought to himself that back home no one would ever believe what the guys had already accomplished. However, little did he know that word was leaked about their exploits and the F.B.I and C.I.A were feverishly at work trying to retrace the seniors' steps hoping to find out what the old guys' final target was. They even paid a visit to the Delightful Donut shop, Jim's daily breakfast stomping grounds, where they found out Jim always held court there with as many as five older gentlemen. The F.B.I then questioned the staff of Delightful Donuts and found out that Jim's discussions occasionally included the owner of the donut shop who happened to have been a Pakistani guy named Stony. This was a red flag! And it could be the break Intelligence needed. Would Stony be able to provide them with information that would lead to the final target?

Minutes later, Stony received a visit from the F.B.I. at his Long Island home. Stony opened the door to see two very official looking men in dark suits. It seemed like an hour before they identified themselves as the F.B.I. Stony's mind was racing. Why would the F.B.I. be interested in him? He was in the country legally and very involved with the Republican party, mostly as a fundraiser for some of the local politicians. He was truly trying to be a good American. The youngest of the two agents started the questioning. He asked Stony if he ever heard of Jim Canova. Stony looked at the agent blankly as beads of sweat formed on his brow. The agent continued .. "You know, the guy you sometime have coffee with at your donut shop?"

Stony's heart began to pound as he had flashbacks of his

conversations with Jim that raced through his head like electric shocks. Now he realized why the agents were there, but what could Jim possibly have done? Jim was a nice older man who just had a very curious mind and liked to ask questions and then Stony thought, and I answered almost all of them. Just then, his thoughts were interrupted by the older agent.

"Do you want to tell us what some of those discussions were about. Your friend Jim is in a lot of trouble and unless you tell us the truth about what you and he have discussed, you too, will be in deep trouble." the officer warned Stony.

Stony felt like he had just been kicked in the balls. His words to Jim shot through his head. (*Jim, if I didn't know better and you weren't so old, I'd think you were a spook!*)

Stony realized he had no choice but to tell the agents everything; all the conversations he had with Jim including Pakistan, his brother being a member of the I.S.I. and Bin Laden's whereabouts. The agents looked at each other and knew they had hit pay dirt. The C.I.A. was immediately notified about the evidence that pointed to the final target being a military base of the Pakistani border. It was all beginning to make sense. This guy Jim had to be the ringleader. But how did these social security recipients ever think they could pull it off? The C.I.A. knew, not only did they think they could pull it off, they were pulling it off unless they could somehow be stopped.

58. LET'S GO TO THE TAPE!

Bin Laden had just recorded a new propaganda tape to be sent to President Obama and it wasn't To Obama, With Love From Usama. Instead, it was a chilling message promising many terrorist attacks in the future. This time, he mentioned big cities, sporting events, transportation and American bases everywhere. At the time of the tape's release, the Pakistani generals were becoming more and more uneasy. It was a fact that the Drone Missiles were getting closer and closer and now they had been notified of an unidentified plane that may be heading their way. They did decide that very soon Bin Laden would have to be moved.

These generals had foreshadowing thoughts that they were about to pay the piper. They did not in their wildest imagination think that the end might possibly be brought on by eight old guys who four months ago, the most exciting thing in their lives was picking up their grandchildren or having Saturday morning breakfast with their old crew.

59. AND ON THE RIGHT

As the guys approached the Arabian Sea, Fred was like a tour guide.

"On the left," he said, "was Yemen and on the right is Somalia."

When Tom heard Somalia, he said, "I would love to drop a little bit of our product on those fucking Somali pirates!"

Fred remarked, "If it was up to you, there would be nothing left for our main target."

The guys were now over the Arabian Sea and heading toward the Pakistan-Afghanistan border. Fred called all the guys up front where they could hear him. He spoke about the parachutes and the likely fuel problem. He said he would give a quick, five-minute course on how to deploy a parachute if any of the guys thought they'd rather take their chances on the ground.

Initially, all the guys said, "No!" Fred then explained that they all did what they had to. The rest of the mission could be taken care of by just two of them, so if they would parachute out, they would probably have a much better chance of survival.

At this point, Jim told the guys, "With the fuel running out, the plan was to crash the plane into the military base."

Dom replied, "I guess we all knew it would come to that."

The guys now entered Pakistani air space and they lost the cover of the water and they were now over land, which made them more vulnerable. They had to fly at a higher altitude because of the mountains. They now were exposed, but even they didn't know how exposed they were! They would very soon find out.

60. WE ARE NOT ALONE

The Pakistani Air Force scrambled three JF17 Thunder Fighters to patrol the Western Afghanistan-Pakistan border and pay special notice to the military base. The young Paki pilots were given the description of the Lear jet that had been given to their Intelligence. The pilots were eager for confrontation and best of all, the plane they were hunting had no way of firing back at them and their orders were to destroy.

The Paki pilots were receiving instructions from their base. The rogue plane was now picked up on the radar and the young pilots were on their way to confront this target of unknowns. They couldn't be more than fifteen minutes west of them.

61. MODERN MEDICINE STINKS

Beletta was notified the Paki Air Force picked up the old guys plane on their radar and was scrambling to intercept them. Two minutes before that, Belleta had ordered the special forces to attack Bin Laden at the refuge the Paki generals had moved them to. The fact that some of the focus was now on the seniors could be a blessing in disguise, of course it could also be a big problem. Beletta at this moment did not need any of the above. Now! His focus was not only on the most evil man in the world, but also on how to save these old fools. He thought to himself, "If it wasn't for modern medicine, half of those old guys would-n't be here." He quickly ordered his people to notify the Pakis that the United States Air Force would intercept their target and escort it out of Paki territory. American planes scrambled off their aircraft carrier in a frantic effort to intercept the 'rogue plane' as it was now being called.

62. IS FRED GOING TO MAKE IT?

Jim did not like the way Fred looked and was reminded of what Fred's doctor had told Fred (That he wasn't a candidate for long-term life insurance). But Fred seemed to have 9 lives. If by some miracle they got out of this, Fred's new name would be cat.

63. PLANES TO THE LEFT, PLANES TO THE RIGHT

Jim asked Fred how he felt. Fred said, "Mommy, stop asking me how I feel every five minutes". "Okay", Jim said "How about answering this, how much fuel do we have left?". "Lets put it this way", Fred said. "Maybe if we were at ground zero in Manhattan, we'd have just enough fuel to get to the far reaches of Connecticut. Maybe 125 miles", Fred added. Just then, almost at the same time, they both spotted the Paki planes on the left. "Oh shit!" They both said practically at the same time. Fred thought to himself, "We are Fucked". Just then, Jim looked to the right and saw American jet fighters, and the Paki jets seemed to melt away.

64. I SMELL A RAT

Beletta was informed that the special forces were now in the compound that housed Bin Laden. They had been in their forty minutes, and it was reported to Beletta that they got Bin Laden, code name, 'The Rat'. The special forces had gone into the compound, guns blazing, and killed Bin Laden and were already on their way back to Afghanistan. Now, Beletta had to figure out immediately how to get the old guys out of Pakistani air space, and to safety. At this time, the old guys were aware that this was not ending the way it was supposed to end. The young American squadron leader bellowed over the two way radio, "Grandpa's, your mission is over". All the guys looked at each other in stunned silence. Jim then grabbed the mic, and said, " It's over when we say it's over, and right now, it's not over!". The young squadron leader comes back with, "You know, we have been ordered to stop you, one way or the other". Jim yells back, "Are you saying you will shoot us down?". "I'm not saying that but you can figure it out" the squadron leader replied. "Besides, I've been told to tell you that your mission was accomplished, only not by you, but by the special forces". Jim comes back again and says, "Are you saying you got Bin Laden?". "I can't say that 100 percent, but it's a good assumption. But either way old man, we have to get you out of Paki air space. My squadron will escort you to Afghanistan." "How far is that?", Jim asked. "less than 100 miles across the Paki-Afghan border", comes the reply. Jim look at the guys. Tom screams, "We can't trust anybody! How can we believe these guys?". Dom says, "Look Tom, it's one thing giving our lives to get Bin Laden, but

quite another thing to get shot down by our fellow Americans."
The mic was left on, and the young squadron leader heard
everything. He then said, "We are not asking anymore". Jim then
looked and saw that they were in the middle of the American jet
squadron. Fred seemed to have perked up. Dom was looking
forward to seeing all the Dominic's and the Dominique's again.
Nelson said, "No matter what happen from here on in, they all
should be very proud of themselves". Phil thought to himself, "
It's amazing, I'll probably live to 100 now". The only one that
was besides himself was Tom. "We came here to do a job, and
we didn't finish it", he screamed. "How do we know that they
are giving us the truth? And have any of you geniuses thought
about what they are going to do to us? We have broken just
about every law, both domestic and international. What if they
decide to make an example out of us?" Tom had raised some
good points. Jim grabbed the mic and said, "Squadron leader
come in, you wont have any resistance from us. But let me ask
you, would you have blown us out of the air?". "I don't have to
answer that now" came the reply, "Do I?". The planes landed at
a make shift Air-Force base in Afghanistan, and the old boys
were escorted to a debriefing area where they then learned that
Bin Laden was definitely dead. They also learned that he wasn't
at the military base they were targeting. He had been moved
two weeks before to a walled compound not 300 yards from the
military base. The C.I.A. had been monitoring every move he
made and that was how the special forces were able to accomplish their goal in less than forty minutes. The President and the
director of the C.I.A. were basking in their success, when
Beletta turned to the President and said, "Mr. President, what
are we going to do with the Q-tips?". They had now officially
been given the code name. 'Q-tips'. C.I.A. director Beletta reasoned to the President, "they created havoc in Libya and almost
jeopardized our plan of attack on Bin Laden". The President
replied, " They actually accelerated it. You know, what they did
was not all bad. Maybe misguided, but not all bad. If we had not
acted when we did, who knows how things would have turned
out?". The old guys were still in Afghanistan one week after they
were forced down. The President had left it in the director

hands as to what their fate would be. Belleta met with his agents, and reviewed everything that had happened. "These misguided patriotic guys were at best vigilantes", he thought. "They had reeked havoc in Libya, violated international law, so how could he let them go unpunished?". On the other hand, the director felt a certain affection for these guys. After all, hadn't Beletta and these old guys shared the same goal? And like it or not, acted together and were part of the same successful ending? The President also seemed to have softened his feelings about them. The Director decided to meet with them in Afghanistan, and hoped maybe he would get some type of epiphany as to what to do with them. The meeting took place on May 10th. Beletta met and liked all the old guys. They were very patriotic, multiethnic, and really everything America was about. They even had a certain amount of street smarts that you couldn't teach. One of them however, had given him a stare that went right through him. Beletta left the meeting thinking eventually he would have to bring these guys back to the states, and maybe even set them free. But then he though, " How could I set them free? Eventually one of them would talk and alert the entire world as to what really happened. How could I guarantee their silence", he thought. Dom started to yell at Tom, "What are you giving the head of the C.I.A. hard looks for? Don't you wanna get outta here?". Tom fired back, "You don't really think they are going to let us go FREE?". "Good question", Jim thought. "Were they viewing us as allies or criminals?". After all the director was going to have to answer questions from other countries on how he could let these guys go unpunished? Phil observed, "They have to let us go". Jim then remarked, "Have any of you guys thought about what's going on with our families at home? Someone has had to have contacted them by now and maybe even told them of our exploits." "Breakfast with Jim", Dom said. "That is the book I am going to write if we ever get out of here alive".

59. A LITTLE BIRD TOLD ME

Beletta returned home to the states to handle all the details made necessary by the killing of Bin Laden. Meanwhile another week had passed, and no decision was yet made on what to do with the old guys. Little did the old boys know that Beletta's people were monitoring every word that they were saying. And when Beletta was notified of Dom's casual reference of Dom writing a book, the hairs on the back of his neck stood at attention. "There can be no books!", Beletta thought. "The part these guys played in the operation must never be found out. They were almost making it impossible to set them free". Beletta's thoughts were giving him headaches. He was starting to play the 'What-if' game. What if he thought, "One of these guys die under the C.I.A. protection?". He knew he had to make a decision quickly. Beletta went to his home that night determined to have a solution by the morning. As he walked into his house, his wife and daughter were watching some brainless program called "Mafia Princess's". "That's it", he thought. "Maybe put these old guys in a program that gives them a new identity, and move them to an area in the United States where they can't possibly be known. We can create a story that we don't know who these guys were who's plane crashed in Afghanistan, and that their remains were too charred to identify. This would mean that having their plane found destroyed in Afghanistan, this could easily be done." This way, Beletta would not have to deal with the international community, where some countries may ask for some type of prosecution.

65. ANOTHER SALES PITCH

Beletta thought, he must handle this himself. He asked the President for the use of Air-Force one, and within 24 hours, was headed back to Afghanistan. "What if these old geezers turned me down", he thought. Then he reasoned, "They were willing to give up their lives to get Bin Laden, at least now he would be offering them the rest of their lives, with their wives as guests of the government, only with new identities". They would have to live in anonymity, and above all, no books. Air-Force One touched down in Afghanistan, and Beletta went right to the compound where the Q-tips were. He had requested a private room and a banquet of food along with some wine, to soften the old guys up. As he entered the room with the six rebels with a cause, he was again greeted with a cold stare from Tom. Dom noticed it and nudged Tom. "Stop it!', he said, "or we might die here". Beletta greeted the Q-tips warmly and said he had something to ask of them, but only after they had eaten. Jim wondered, "Are they fattening us up for they kill?".

66. TILL DEATH DO US PART

The food was great, but it was tempered by what was coming next. They ate, they drank, and even shared a laugh with Beletta. Then Beletta turned serious, and began to set the guys up. "Gentlemen", he said, "No one doubts your patriotism or your love for America. After all, you were ready to give your lives for your country. Your country, your President, and myself are all very proud of all of you. No one would ever believe what you have accomplished. What you did however, must be our little secret. We cannot afford to let the rest of the world know of what you did. Your president and myself, have agreed to relocate you guys and your wives to a new location." Tommy looked at the rest of the guys, and blurted out, "The fucking witness protection program! They're gonna put us in the witness protection program like we are some kind of criminals!" "Not exactly my cold-staring friend. But you will be our guests for the rest of your lives complete with new identities, and a generous amount of money. All of your activities however, will be closely monitored. You will soon be joined here by your two pals, Steve and Billy. They are being picked up as we speak". Jim said, "Can we have some time to discuss this?". Beletta replied firmly, "There is no discussion, you remain here or you take our generous offer. Can you ask for anything more in view of what you've done? Your medical, a pension, a house, all will be provided for you. You will all become guests of the government for the rest of your lives. Just two weeks ago, you were ready to throw your lives away without even knowing if you would accomplish your mission. Now you know that Bin Laden is dead, and the government will take care of you and your wives for the rest of your lives.? "The Fucking witness protection program!", Tommy yelled. Beletta just looked at Tom, this time it was him who gave the cold stare. Dom looked at Tom and said, "Shutup". Beletta wondered how much of a thorn this ex-marine Tom was going to be. Beletta decided to stay overnight and visit again with the Q-tips in the morning.

67. MASS CONFUSION

Meanwhile back home in America, the headlines and news bulletins were still unfolding about Bin Laden. It seems like one every five minutes. The Q-tips wives were huddled together at Jim's home, worried and confused. "Had the Bin Laden demise involved their husbands? Could that even be possible?" The phones were ringing off the hook. The front bell rang. As Jim's wife opened the door she saw two well-dressed gentlemen. The older of the two identified himself and asked if he could please come in. As he looked around, he seemed to have known that all the wives would have been there. He then asked them to please follow him. "Why", asked Marie, Dom's wife. The man replied, "Because I'm going to take you to see your husbands. All of the woman were startled and Joyce, Billy's wife asked to see identification. 10 minutes later, a long-black limousine was seen leaving Oceanside. The women looked to the left and to the right watching the trees go by and the water pass as they left. They wondered in what condition would they find their husbands. As the Limo headed towards the Southern State Parkway, they noticed it was a clear sunny day. But little did they know, this was the last time that they would be seeing Long Island.

68. "I'VE HAD IT"

Beletta thought there had to be an easier job for him in the administration. The last few weeks had aged him ten years. The actions of those old bastards he thought, were actually necessary to the success of the special forces. Beletta also knew however that he had to make them disappear. After all they broke every law both domestically and internationally. He didn't like the term witness-protection program, which would imply that they were gangsters. But in reality, the old ex-marine was right, it was a witness protection program. When Beletta had interrogated the old guys, he was sure at least seven of them were not gangsters. Maybe bored old men, but maybe honest to god heroes. Yes that's it Beletta thought, they really were heroes. After all, they were willing to give up their lives for their country, isn't that one of the definitions of heroes. Probably, the oldest heroes he had ever been involved with. Heroes nonetheless. Beletta remembered hearing one of them say, "What do we have to lose? We are on Bonus time".